The
Accidental
AFTERLIFE
of
Thomas
Marsden

Also by Emma Trevayne

Flights and Chimes and Mysterious Times

The
Accidental
AFTERLIFE
of
Thomas
Marsden

EMMA TREVAYNE

Simon & Schuster Books for Young Readers
NEW YORK   LONDON   TORONTO   SYDNEY   NEW DELHI

SIMON & SCHUSTER BOOKS FOR YOUNG READERS

An imprint of Simon & Schuster Children's Publishing Division

1230 Avenue of the Americas, New York, New York 10020

Text copyright © 2015 by Emma Trevayne

Jacket Illustration copyright © 2015 by Glenn Thomas

SIMON & SCHUSTER BOOKS FOR YOUNG READERS is a trademark of Simon & Schuster, Inc.

For information about special discounts for bulk purchases, please contact Simon & Schuster Special Sales at 1-866-506-1949 or business@simonandschuster.com.

The Simon & Schuster Speakers Bureau can bring authors to your live event. For more information or to book an event, contact the Simon & Schuster Speakers Bureau at 1-866-248-3049 or visit our website at www.simonspeakers.com.

Jacket design by Lizzy Bromley

Interior design by Hilary Zarycky

The text for this book is set in Granjon.

Manufactured in the United States of America

0615 FFG

2 4 6 8 10 9 7 5 3 1

Library of Congress Cataloging-in-Publication Data

Trevayne, Emma.

The accidental afterlife of Thomas Marsden / Emma Trevayne.—1st edition.

pages cm

Summary: At age twelve, grave robber Thomas Marsden discovers a boy who looks just like him in an unmarked grave and begins a journey of discovery as he learns of faeries trapped in London and their hope that he can return them to their realm.

ISBN 978-1-4424-9882-2 (hardcover)

ISBN 978-1-4424-9886-0 (eBook)

[1. Identity—Fiction. 2. Fairies—Fiction. 3. Magic—Fiction. 4. Changelings—Fiction. 5. Spiritualists—Fiction. 6. Grave robbing—Fiction. 7. London (England)—History—19th century—Fiction. 8. Great Britain—History—Victoria, 1837–1901—Fiction.] I. Title.

PZ7.T73264Acc 2015

[Fic]—dc23

2014032574

FIRST
EDITION

To J. G. and A. R.,
with all the love and gratitude
in this world or any other

And also with pineapples

ACKNOWLEDGMENTS

Different books grow from idea to novel in different ways. *Afterlife* was determined to surprise me at every turn; the only thing that never changed was its title. As much as I would like to claim I weathered those surprises through sheer force of will, in reality it was thanks to the support of the following people:

My family, particularly those who instilled a love of reading and words in me from such an early age.

Brooks Sherman. I could probably write books without the best agent ever, but I wouldn't want to.

Zareen Jaffery. For any author, an editor who just *gets* you and what you're trying to say is important. To have one who is also insightful, generous, understanding, brilliant, kind, and funny is a lottery win.

All the amazing people at Simon & Schuster Books for Young Readers, especially Mekisha for being awesomely organized when I'm not (which is most of the time), and Lizzy and Hilary for a beautiful book.

Glenn Thomas, who once again turned my words into stunning visual art.

A novel's worth of lovely, hilarious, strange-in-awesome-ways characters who are as essential to my success as the faeries are to Mordecai's: Heidi Schulz, Stefan Bachmann, Claire Legrand, Katherine Catmull, and Alice Viccajee. Leiah, for keeping me supplied with sugar. My Strings, who know who they are.

Lastly, and perhaps most importantly, you. You who are holding this book and giving up your precious time to read it, you who may have read about weird music or magic birds and agreed to join me on another dark adventure. Thank you.

CHAPTER ONE

Bones

T HOMAS MARSDEN WAS ELEVEN YEARS old when
he dug up his own grave.

It was the twenty-ninth day of April, though
for only another few moments, and thus he would be eleven
years old for only another few moments. When he awoke
next morning, there'd be a tiny honey cake beside his bowl
of gruel, and he'd give himself one bite each day until it
was gone. The previous year, he'd managed to make it last
near a week.

Midnight was clear and bright, with a hint of summer
in the spring, and the headstones glowed like a mouthful
of teeth under the moon. This was a messy business in the
rain, so at least there was that. Thomas's fingers curled

around the shovel's handle as he looked back and forth across the plots, waiting for one to speak to him, just as he'd been taught.

When he was smaller, it'd been Thomas's job to keep watch, eyes and ears peeled for anyone who might have it in mind to stop them. There'd been some close ones, but nobody'd ever caught them.

But for a while now, Thomas'd been old enough to dig.

Behind him, his father waited. Waited to see if Thomas "had the bones." That's what Silas Marsden called it, the sense of knowing which grave might hold the plunder that would feed them, keep the tallow candles burning another while.

The yew trees cast shadows of tall, dark ghosts waving gnarled arms and shaking wild, leafy heads. Stars peered through, bright, watching eyes, blinking in horror at the desecration that was about to come.

But stars knew nothing of empty bellies and grates with no coal. Stars always had fire.

"Hurry up, then," grizzled Silas. "Find your bones, or I will."

That wouldn't do. Silas was always just a bit more generous when Thomas did the work—and happier to have someone else to blame if they caught a dud.

Thomas turned this way and that, and froze.

"D'you hear something?" he asked. Footsteps, he was

almost sure of it. The very particular sound of footsteps trying not to make any noise.

Tap, tap, tap, on the soft grass between the graves.

"Don't 'ear nothing. If I didn't know better, I'd think you was frightened. Not frightened, are you, son?"

Thomas straightened his shoulders. He most certainly was *not*. Perhaps it was nothing. Trees or an animal. He never felt alone in graveyards, anyway.

"This way," he said, starting in the opposite direction from whence the possibly imagined footsteps had gone. Shovels over shoulders, they trudged along the paths, sacks in their hands, which would hopefully soon be filled.

Beyond the graveyard walls, the lively, stinking city felt very far away, banished by this land of the dead. Thomas dropped his sack and shovel beside a crumbling stone on which he could just make out the name COSGROVE because Mam had insisted he learn his letters.

In this work, there was always a choice to be made. Older graves might've been turned over already, their treasures taken, but for those as were untouched, what they held could be worth a whole handful of coin. Newer ones were a safe bet for a few bits and bobs, but rare was the one that'd feed them for a month.

The digging itself was no easy job. Sweaty and back-breaking and endless, the blades of the shovels chewing up the earth and diving in for another mouthful, only to spit it out onto a growing hill beside the growing hole. When their arms would no longer reach—sooner for Thomas than his father—Thomas would jump lightly into the grave and try not to think of what was beneath his feet.

And then there was a moment, there was always a moment, when metal struck wood and Thomas could loosen his blistered fingers from the handle, for they were almost finished. This was also the moment when the stench began to waft, a smell of sickness and decay. Thomas covered his nose with a ragged shirtsleeve that, truth be told, didn't smell much better.

Rotted wood splintered under a final blow, and again when Silas climbed down to pull the coffin's lid free of its rusted hinges.

"Not bad," he muttered. "Not so bad at all. This'll fetch a bit from the right buyer if it's polished up right nice." A silver brush, its bristles long since fallen away to dust, gleamed in his hand. Thomas tried quite hard not to look at the spot it had come from, right between two hands that were nothing but bone now, but he could never resist completely.

The whole body was nothing but bone, bone and gaps for mouth and nose, ears and eyes. Two silver coins had fallen with unheard *clunks* to the wood below at some point after it had been buried and forgotten.

"Reckon you can keep one of those," said Thomas's father, as was his way. He was not, by and large, a cruel man, and always gave Thomas a small share of the spoils if Thomas helped. A bigger share, if Thomas chose, and chose well. Most times, Thomas slipped it into his mother's purse so she might return from market with a few extra morsels.

The brush, a music box, the other coin, and a pair of shoe buckles went into a sack. Not bad for a night. Thomas climbed from the grave, his father behind, and they made quick work of filling it back up from the mountain of earth. Oh, by the light of day it would be clear that someone had disturbed the plot, but by then they would be long gone.

"Got time for another." The moon still shone high in the sky.

Soon they wouldn't, as the days grew longer and warmer and stole the darkness that shrouded them. Winter was best. They scarcely had to wait past suppertime, but on those bitter cold days when the ground was frozen solid, it oftentimes took a whole night to dig just one.

Thomas led them deeper into the graveyard, almost to the wall that surrounded it, and near clapped with glee. A fresh one, so new as to not even have a marker yet, no name to read or years at which to wonder. The digging was so much easier when they was fresh, too, the earth loose and unsettled, welcoming the body back into its embrace.

"An easy one, eh? Good job." Thomas's father patted his shoulder with a calloused hand. The objects in the sack clattered together as it hit the ground, and they both readied their shovels.

They did not have to dig far.

And there was no wood to splinter.

A scant few feet down, Thomas's shovel struck something that was surely not a coffin.

"What in blazes—? Careful!"

Thomas dropped to his knees and began to brush the earth away with his hands. The corpse was new, plump and cool, the cloth that covered it whole and perfect. Worms and critters hadn't gotten to it yet.

He swept the last of the dirt from the face, and his blood ran colder than the skin under his fingers. And then, as if it would make some sort of difference, he scooped the earth from the rest of the body in great, messy handfuls. It made no difference at all, no good one, and a dozen feelings all choked in Thomas's throat like a chicken bone, for looking at the body was like . . . like staring into a pond on a clear day.

When Silas Marsden had told Thomas to "find his bones," this was not what was meant, but it might as well have been. In the grave, smeared with earth on skin not covered by a black robe, was Thomas himself, down to the ragged fingernails, the blemish on his cheek, there in a shard of looking glass since Thomas could remember. Silas Marsden whispered a prayer.

There was not a single difference, so far as Thomas could see. True, he was not covered in earth, and his skin was warmer than the soil-smeared face below him, but those things weren't as important as the ones that were exactly the same. The face, the hands, the skinny chest when Silas parted the robe with the end of his shovel. Despite the strangeness before them, it seemed he couldn't resist the urge to make sure there was nothing of value under the cloth.

"I don't understand," said Thomas. "It looks just like me. Why does it look just like me?"

"We bury it again," snapped his father, ignoring Thomas's question, seeming to answer a different one as he looked up at the stars. "Doesn't have nothing to take. We bury it again and get out of 'ere. Come on, quick."

"But—"

"Do as I say, or feel the back of my hand, boy!"

"But it does have something!" said Thomas, startled. Silas had never struck him, not when he spilled his supper or broke a mug or put holes in his jumpers, and he knew many who were not so fortunate. Silas was *afraid*, a thing so unfamiliar to Thomas it took him a heartbeat to see it for what it was.

But he couldn't do as Silas asked, for Silas was wrong.

Thomas pulled free the curl of paper from under the cold fingers that were otherwise identical to his own, and a shiver passed through him, as, briefly, he held his own hand.

Silas peered at it in the moonlight. "What's it say? Read those letters your mam's made you learn. Never saw any call for that, meself."

The ink was so blue it was almost black, formed into whorls and spikes. At first look, they seemed nothing like the letters Mam had painstakingly taught him, sounding each one out and stringing them together into words. He squinted as the shapes seemed to wriggle and change.

"It says, *My name is Thistle,*" Thomas whispered. What an odd name. And what an odd feeling it was that came over Thomas, a wave of despair and fright from the boy at his feet, as clear as if the boy could talk and had whispered to Thomas that he was sad and afraid. Odd. But there was nothing about this that wasn't odd, and the name wasn't the only thing the note said.

Do not read this aloud. Go. Wear a cap. Watch. Speak to no one. This is essential.

Three more bits of paper had fallen to the ground. Thomas gathered them up, and these were printed in ordinary letters. He'd seen something like them once before, when the graves had been particularly rich and Mam had taken him to a penny theater as a treat.

Those tickets hadn't been made of such thick card, however, with gold leaf around the edges. The theater hadn't been in such a posh part of town as the address on these, neither.

The performance was the following night.

"This is all some daft trick," said Silas, gripping his shovel tighter, the distraction over. "Get to work."

Thomas slipped the note and the tickets into his pocket.

Calluses burned on Thomas's palm. He tipped the first load of earth slowly back into the hole, where it covered the face so like his own. Another shovel of dirt, slowly again. But his pace did not matter, for Silas Marsden worked as if possessed, scooping up huge clumps and throwing them into the grave, breath labored and loud in the quiet night.

He did not say another word to Thomas, not when they had finished, nor on the long trudge home, nor when he pushed open the creaking door and pointed in the direction of Thomas's small bed, really no more than a pile of moth-eaten blankets near the hearth.

If there was coal, Mam always left a few embers glowing for the bit of warmth that stole over Thomas as he climbed under the topmost blanket—the thinnest and most threadbare. The others formed a nest underneath him that softened the hard floor. Most nights he was weary, tired to his very bones from hours in the graveyards, and grateful to fall asleep soon as he was burrowed in, but not this night.

Tonight his bones in this bed couldn't be as tired as his bones in the grave, so exhausted they would never move again.

It simply made no sense, not the slightest bit. The Robertsons down the road and round the corner, they had two girls, twins, who looked so much the same that Thomas couldn't tell which was waving to him in the street. But Mam and Papa had never so much as hinted at Thomas having a brother. He longed to ask his father, longed right up until the moment Silas Marsden finished hanging up coats and shovels on the nails by the door and stomped across the room in socks badly in need of darning. The door to the house's one other room slammed shut hard enough to wake Mam, asleep on the other side.

Sure enough, voices slipped like smoke through the cracks around the wood. Whispers, and they got no louder even when Thomas crept from his bed to press his ear against the rough, splintery planks. The floor was cold under his toes, drafts breathed across his neck, but Thomas did not move except to sit when his legs would no longer hold him.

When Thomas woke, he was in his bed, warm, the fire ablaze in the hearth. A long spoon clanged on the side of a metal pot hung over the flames on a hook.

"Wake up. That's your breakfast ready," said Thomas's mother. "Come now, eat." She looked tired, great dark circles under her eyes, but she was smiling as always. Her hair curled in wisps over her shawl.

"In the graveyard—" Thomas began, remembering.

"There's clean water. Wash your hands, as I can guess you didn't before bed, and I won't have you getting my spoons mucky. Those as has an 'undred of them can get them as filthy as they likes, but not in this home, I say."

Perhaps she would let him ask his questions if he did as he was bade. This was quite often the case with Mam, who got more kindly with each completed chore. Thomas had learned this very young.

He wrested himself from the nest of blankets, which had become nearly too hot under the wash of warmth from the blazing fire and dipped his hands into the bucket in the corner. Too cold. Everything was always either too warm or too cold, usually the latter. His gruel this morning burned his tongue, though, and Thomas was sure Mam had cooked it much longer than usual as he'd slept. The honey cake sat in a chipped dish, but Thomas had more important things to think about.

"Last night—"

Thomas's mother began to whistle as she scrubbed the shelves that held their cups and bowls.

She told him off for whistling. Said it was rude.

"Where's Papa?"

Finally, Lucy Marsden met Thomas's eyes. "Gone out," she said, knuckles clenched white around the rag in her fist. "Said 'e'd be back soon, and that there'd be a bit of pie for us to have for lunch. I know as you both found something strange last night, but I won't discuss it, not without your—not without Silas 'ere. So you be a good boy and do today's lesson, and we'll just wait."

Thomas knew two things: that there was something he wasn't being told, and that Mam, having made her mind up good and proper, wouldn't tell him no matter how he begged.

So he'd had a brother once. Surely that was it. A brother down to an identical birthmark, and even the Robertson girls didn't have those, far as Thomas knew. Not that he'd ever asked, or had reason to.

It wasn't so odd, really, to foster out a child. Where would another have slept in this house? On the nights there was no food at all, even bread or old potatoes filched from the barrow-man, one less mouth to feed must've seemed a blessing.

But now his brother was in a grave, and an empty, uneasy feeling slithered through Thomas from his belly to his fingers and toes.

It was the nature of the Marsden business, if it could be called a business, that Thomas had seen far more than his fair share of cold, unbreathing bodies and skeletons rotting to dust. The boy in the grave, however, he had looked healthy, as if the pinkness had been only temporarily stolen from his cheeks and would return any moment.

Thomas shivered. He could not finish the gruel in his bowl, just thinking about it. Mam didn't even tell him to finish up, simply took his breakfast away and replaced it with a book as if it were a day like any other, when it was anything but. Heavy, worn, the long words faded and sometimes missing where the pages were torn right out. The firelight flickered across the paper and, behind Thomas, his mother dusted things that were already as clean and tidy as they'd ever get in this dank, sooty room.

Click-thunk.

At the sound of his father's boots on the doorstep, Thomas straightened, and Mam dropped her cloth. Hinges creaked and Silas Marsden stepped in, flushed and sweaty, hands holding a twist of greasy brown paper that he set on the end of the table.

"All right?" Mam asked.

"Aye." But Silas did not sound all right. His voice was quiet, even gruffer than usual. He fixed his eyes on Thomas.

"We need to have a chat, boy. Some things your—some things we should've told ye before now."

Thomas could smell the pie, with real meat in it. Well, it

was his birthday. "I had a brother," he said, expecting them both to agree. But his father grimaced, and his mother folded her hands together.

"That may well be," said Silas. "Truth is, we wouldn't rightly know. See, there we was, muddling along, just the two of us. Never no babies on the way, and that's just how it was. But your mam, she wanted one, and I could see the . . . the advantages, ye might say, of having someone could learn the skills of the trade I've picked up in my time. Funny business, grave robbing. Got to treat it with respect. You get what's you deserve. Go out there with a smile on your face and a shovel in your hand, and there might be riches. Dig as if you were digging to the devil 'imself, and you'll find nothing but dirt."

Before he could open his mouth, Thomas's mother spoke. "What your papa means to say is that, well, we sort of found you, a bit."

"Found me?" Thomas asked, blinking. "Where?"

Though he had been red just a few minutes before, Silas's face paled in the licking orange light from the hearth. "That's just the thing," he said, almost to himself. "We found you in a grave, too. *On* one, really, curled up against the headstone and quiet as a ghost."

CHAPTER TWO

The First Test

TWO PAIRS OF EYES HAD watched Thomas and Silas enter the graveyard.

"He looked just—" said the younger one.

"Hush."

They had watched the discovery, and watched Thomas and Silas leave again, the fear and confusion on their faces so obvious in the bright moonlight. Relief filled the elder one as the boy read the note. A promising start.

"I don't understand why we can't just find him and tell him, Deadnettle," said the younger, when it was safe once more to speak.

The tall, old one named Deadnettle had sighed. He had, indeed, asked himself this very question, and ruled it impossible for a great many reasons. Not only impossible, but foolish, too. In his pocket, his fingers turned over the small, corked bottle of ink.

"He must come to us," said Deadnettle calmly. "He must prove himself capable of that much, at least."

"You're testing him? Now? You wanted to see if he could read the note, didn't you?"

"Yes. There are things I must know about him. Whether he is clever, and whether he can do as he is told. Whether he is as kind as his mother and—this is the most important thing, Marigold—whether he can be trusted with a secret so large."

"We're going to watch him," Marigold said, with no hint of question.

"We are. Not for long. We do not have long." A week, perhaps. No more. He pushed the thought away and smiled slightly. "Also, I would like for you to imagine how you might react, if you were Thomas and I were simply to approach you on the street and tell you the truth."

Marigold considered this. She laughed, and then she frowned. "I see. But if reading the note is as much as he can do?"

"Then, Marigold . . ."

But there was no *then*. Then Deadnettle would not know what to do. Even this much was a risk, a last, desperate chance, taken only because his beloved Wintercress, whom he had always held to be right in all things, had been so very wrong.

The graveyard had scarcely changed since the night, twelve years earlier, when Deadnettle had placed the tiny infant Thomas on a well-tended grave and waited in these same shadows for someone to find him. He hadn't been *Thomas* then. He hadn't been anything. The unimportant one. But Deadnettle hadn't wanted him to perish, and neither had Wintercress. She had told him what to do, and so he'd kept watch until Silas Marsden found the creature and took it home, Deadnettle following at a safe distance.

He'd watched there, too, for a time. And then he had returned to care for the kept one.

The important one.

He had taught Thistle all he knew, at least up to the point when Thistle's powers had surpassed Deadnettle's own, and the pupil became the master. From before that, however, Deadnettle had many a memory of schooling Thistle in the ways of faery, and in how to act human when such a distasteful act was required. He'd watched Thistle grow, heard his ready laugh shape into an echo of Wintercress's, touched his hair when Deadnettle said they were finished with magical practice for the night but Thistle, exhausted and determined, begged for one more lesson.

Perhaps if I had given them, thought Deadnettle sadly, *perhaps if I had let him practice more, instead of forcing him to rest, we would not be here.*

Marigold had wandered over to the fresh grave—she'd done most of the digging, to save Deadnettle's waning strength—and stared down.

He'd given her a moment. The boy within had been her closest friend, and it was the more surprising, therefore, how quickly she'd accepted the whole truth. Much more quickly than Thomas would, that was a certainty, but Marigold hadn't lived eleven years believing herself to be human.

Telling her had meant breaking a solemn promise, one made in the moments before Wintercress had used her last rush of magic and, because of that, drawn her last breath. But, in her way, Wintercress had broken a promise to him too, so perhaps letting Marigold in on this long-kept secret was the proper choice.

The only choice. Deadnettle was no longer strong enough to have carried out the night's task alone. Ah, he envied her the energy of the young. Marigold and the other fledglings were not yet as weak, as sick as the rest of them, who had been fully grown when they'd come to London.

A smile, bitter as lemons. *Come.* As if it had been voluntary. As if they had wanted to, and not been dragged to this filthy city, with its biting, stinging, poisoning iron everywhere one looked and ringing church bells everywhere one listened.

An angry red burn crossed Marigold's palm where she'd grasped the iron graveyard gate.

"Come," Deadnettle had finally said. "We must go back."

"I don't want to. I never want to."

"I know," he'd answered, but he was surprised—not at her words, but that she'd said them. Usually she was the cheeriest of them, despite little cause to be. She had just lost her friend; he must remember that. The three of them had been aware of the risk, but even so, none had wanted to believe the worst would happen. He looked her straight in her pretty face. Fledglings so easily passed for human—or, the more beautiful sort of human, of which there weren't many. It was not until later that the signs began to show. In the moonlight she'd seemed just a girl, and he flinched, momentarily afraid of what she saw when she looked at him.

Age and frailty, for certain. Both were more than true.

"Come," he had said again. "We must be back before dawn." Because of Mordecai, of course, and the time Deadnettle could stand to be out among the metal was getting shorter and shorter. He could last only a few hours now at most.

This time she did not argue. They'd approached the high, ornate gates, nothing like the gate through which they had been hoping to make their final escape. Marigold's muffled scream as she grasped the metal pained him near as much as it did her.

"Will Mordecai wonder what's happened to him?" Marigold asked, speaking the name as she might a curse.

"He was younger than most of our lost ones, it's true." Deadnettle himself was concerned about this, but nothing could be done now. "I will simply say that Thistle was clearly overworked, and that we have cared for him as we do all our dead. Do not worry."

"But—"

"Do not worry."

"And what will we tell the others?"

"The same."

"Nothing about . . . Thomas?"

"Not yet. We will tell them when—*if*—there is reason to hope. To do otherwise would be cruel."

They walked through the streets, Deadnettle's face shielded by the hood of his cloak. In this part of the city, the houses and shops huddled close together as if for warmth, too few of them lit by hearth fires within. Cracked cobbles slipped beneath their feet, and everywhere a nose-wrinkling stench.

Marigold dropped a few steps behind, and Deadnettle thought he heard a soft, quiet sob. Perfectly understandable. Simply because he had never been able to force tears for Wintercress didn't mean Marigold shouldn't cry for Thistle. He had left her to it, trusting her to skip back to his side when ready, and concentrated on ignoring the iron. Which was impossible. It couldn't be dismissed as a mere nuisance, but trying was preferable to surrender. Sputtering gas lamps and fences and the signs over shop windows, it was everywhere. Poison, sapping his strength with every step, draining his senses so his vision blurred and he could no longer hear—

"Marigold?" He spun round. "Marigold!"

Her cloak flashed around a corner, streaming behind her. Oh, the energy of the fledglings! Their health! Quick as he could, Deadnettle chased, a sinking sensation dizzying him.

They were not far. "No!" he shouted, but he could not do so loudly, for fear of awakening the street and someone who might peer from a window at the inhuman face below, its hood blown off by the wind as he ran.

He heard her scream, louder and more agonized than when she'd opened the graveyard gate. She lay in the middle of the road when he reached her, thrown back by the force of the boundary they could not cross. It encircled London, powerful against them as an iron ring, though it could not be seen nor grasped.

"I'm fine!" she hissed, jumping to her feet, far too enraged for pain, and Deadnettle envied her this, too. He could remember feeling the same, long ago. "I want to go home! Thistle said he was strong enough. He *promised* me he was strong enough to try!"

"And he should have been." *Oh, Wintercress,* Deadnettle thought, *how could you have been so wrong?* "You saw him cover the sun with the moon. Wintercress said that was how we would know he was ready, that he had reached full strength. It is not our fault that . . . It is not our fault."

"I want to go home," she repeated, and it was not the time to remind her that she spoke of a home she had never seen, and that the memories she had heard spoken by her elders were in danger of passing into myth by virtue of time, becoming nothing more than stories, bedtime tales.

"We all do," Deadnettle said. "No one more than I, Marigold. It is a powerful enchantment we are under. Mordecai is skilled, and we are weak. Thistle was the strongest of us, but even that, even that was not enough."

"Is there nothing that will break it?"

Deadnettle paused. "No. Thomas is our only hope now." He could be certain, at least, that Thomas existed. He was their only chance.

And not much of one at that. There was a very good reason Deadnettle had put him on that grave years before, cast
out as a useless thing. Blood and time were against them.
Time, because after tonight, the worlds would drift apart
again. They had a week, perhaps, until the gap would be
too large to leap.

Overhead, the pinkness of morning had touched the
sky. Deadnettle clasped Marigold's hand firmly in his own
and together they walked north once more, amid the sting
of iron and fear, trapped within the city that enclosed them
like a fist.

Long after Marigold had curled up on a fetid mattress,
Deadnettle kept his drooping eyes open, deep in thought.

He would have to be very careful, more so than ever
before, while taking greater risks. It might be simpler,
perhaps, if he was certain the boy could—or would—help
them. Deadnettle had no knowledge of what kind of child
Thomas was, having paid him no more attention over
the past eleven years than necessary to keep track of
the boy's whereabouts. And that only because he felt he
ought to. Worthless and watery though it was, Thomas
remained Wintercress's blood. The very last drops of an
ancient, noble line ran through his veins.

Deadnettle looked around the dank cellar, water and

slime coating the walls. This was no palace, but it was a haven of sorts.

There was no iron here. Oh, how benevolent Mordecai was. Unconcerned with what the faeries did when he was not using them. Mordecai knew they would always return, if they bothered to leave, and why should they venture out into the city that hurt them so? Even if they dared, they would always keep themselves hidden, for fear someone else might treat them even more shockingly than Mordecai did.

Mordecai was clever. Too clever. Just enough freedom to be a punishment.

Footsteps neared. Deadnettle squinted through the gloom.

"Samphire," he said.

"I've been summoned upstairs." She paused, waiting for Deadnettle to offer himself in her stead. He did this for the hatchlings and fledglings whenever he could, to spare their pain, and because he hoped. He hoped that they would yet see their homeland, and it was the hatchlings and fledglings who would restore their race to what it had once been. Those who were strong enough to birth new hatchlings in this poisoned place were never summoned upstairs. Mordecai and his benevolence once more. That left few but Deadnettle to volunteer; today, he could not.

The night had left him far too drained, and this was exactly the wrong time to make Mordecai suspicious.

The wrong time . . .

"The performance is this evening," said Deadnettle, eyebrows furrowed. "There should be no sessions today. Mordecai always has us rest." Deadnettle would not go so far as to say they were given a holiday on this day every year, merely that their suffering was delayed until nightfall.

Samphire spread her long-fingered hands. She knew no more about Mordecai's activities than Deadnettle. Less, indeed. There were things he was careful not to tell any of the others; they did not need to be frightened or sickened more than they already were.

"Be strong," he told Samphire. "Do as you're bidden."

"Yes, Deadnettle." She retreated, leaving him in his dark, filthy corner to sleep.

He was tired, too tired to allow his strength to be sapped any more today. So tired that *tired* wasn't even the proper word for it. Exhausted down to the marrow of his bones, which were not human bones. Oh, how lovely it would be to sleep long enough that he must never wake; he almost envied Thistle that, comfortable and at peace in his grave.

No. Deadnettle could not allow himself to think like this. He refused, *refused*, to die in this horrid, iron-banded city. And that was the only reason Deadnettle clung to a last scrap of hope—for to abandon it would mean certain defeat, and he might as well close his eyes, concede surrender this very instant.

He pushed himself to his feet and looked around. He had very good vision in the dark. The others lay in varying states of rest, slumbering or something close enough to it that it made hardly any difference. That was good, for two reasons: They weren't paying much attention to him, and they were resting up for the evening. Mordecai's grand celebration.

It was supposed to be Deadnettle's grand celebration, not Mordecai's. But Thistle had failed at the first attempt, the practice.

Mordecai knew the significance of the date. And, Deadnettle supposed, it was a special occasion for himself and the others, too. Thirteen years exactly since they had been brought here.

But things had been so different then. Wintercress had been alive. Deadnettle had been strong.

Marigold was sleeping. Good. He had needed her for the graveyard errand, but this, this he would do alone. The first flower-seed of doubt, of mystery, had been planted in the boy's mind, but it wouldn't grow without nourishment.

Despite what he had said to Marigold, Deadnettle's

plan, if it could be termed such, was as faint and illusory as their chances of returning home. He had not lied to her—he could not do that—but nor did he have a clear path forward. He would watch the boy, yes, but as much to figure out which steps to take as to decide if it was worth taking them for Thomas.

Daylight was a risk. For that matter, so was leaving the cellar, but Samphire was upstairs with Mordecai and whatever group of furred, diamond-crusted society ladies he'd gathered today. And Deadnettle had no intention of using the front door.

Wrapped in his hooded cloak, Deadnettle strode through the streets of London. The trick was to move quickly, give no one a chance to look for too long, to wonder. Above all, it was imperative he not shy from the iron, or scream if he got too close. Behind the patched, scratchy cloth covering his face, Deadnettle gritted long, pointed teeth. He did not listen to the hum of chatter that filled the city. Unlike Marigold, he was not curious. While she still appeared so human, she could come and go among them almost as she liked. And what she liked were the humans' vast lending libraries and bookshops. More than once, Deadnettle had been forced to find her, or send one of the other fledglings if he was too weak himself.

Thistle used to accompany her. He wondered whether

she would venture out alone now, in what he hoped was the short time they had left here.

He slipped past the window of the tiny hovel just as a shadow might, and listened. He had very good hearing, any hour of the day. He didn't have to be anywhere near this close by, but it was . . . soothing . . . to be in the presence of the last of Wintercress's blood, even if Thomas didn't know it.

The bricks at his back were filthy and worn, but Deadnettle didn't give that overmuch thought as he sat down to wait. There were worse places, and the hard, scrabbling lives of the poor humans who dwelled for miles around meant there was little expensive iron to be found. Little, but enough. What there was settled into Deadnettle as a deep, feverish ache, and there was simply the occasional additional sting as someone walked past three streets away with a poker or a pipe.

Silas Marsden's footsteps came from the west, heavy and mean. Deadnettle roused himself and listened, as much to get a sense of the boy as for the information Deadnettle might glean about Thomas's next movements. He did not seem a . . . *bad* child, difficult as it was for Deadnettle to think of humans any other way.

The boy was not precisely human, Deadnettle reminded himself. But he was closer to that than anything else. From what Deadnettle had seen, Thomas did not have the faeries' sensitivity to iron, nor their enhanced senses. He had suspected there was someone in the graveyard with them the previous night, but had he possessed Deadnettle's abilities, there would have been no doubt.

Doubt. Deadnettle was consumed by it. If the boy had no faery skills whatsoever, it was possible he would be able to do nothing for them. It was *likely* he would be able to do nothing for them. If Thomas could not take Thistle's place in the ritual, or if some other way to use him couldn't be found, Thomas would indeed be as useless as a human. He had been raised by them and did not know he could be anything but. Likely, he didn't even know there was another possibility.

He would. Soon. If he was clever enough. And if he wasn't, well, nothing would ever matter again.

The sound of Silas Marsden's boots arrived before the scent or sight of him did, and Deadnettle had plenty of time to press himself into the shadows of sunset before Silas neared the house. He listened to the man enter, to the conversation that began and the questions Thomas asked of his parents. Or at least, the people he had believed to be his parents until this moment.

The true story . . . Deadnettle hoped to tell him that in good time. He was being told part of it now, not by

Deadnettle himself but by Silas and Lucy: the tale of the night they found him in the graveyard.

Deadnettle listened, but not with much interest. He knew all of this already.

"So you don't know where I came from, or who would've left my brother for me to find."

Deadnettle's ears pricked. It didn't take much cleverness to guess that Thistle had been put there for a reason, but it was a positive sign. *He was not your brother, child,* he wanted to say, but this wasn't the moment. If he must, he would do exactly what he'd told Marigold he couldn't— stop the boy in the street and tell him everything. But it wouldn't come to that. Inside the hovel, paper was rustling. Not cheap pulp, but good, thick card, with gold leaf around the edges.

"They left me these," said Thomas. "Must've done it for a reason."

"A séance?" Silas Marsden scoffed. "What, you supposed to go natter to the ghost of your poor brother, ask who put 'im in that hole?"

Deadnettle couldn't see Thomas's face, and he could not read minds. He hazarded, however, that Thomas was giving this idea due consideration. Well, this was the first test. Would the boy do as Deadnettle had instructed in the note, and not speak to anyone?

It was *essential* that he stay silent and hidden as possible. If Mordecai glimpsed him, there was no telling what might happen next.

But then, if Thomas couldn't follow a simple instruction, it didn't much matter.

"P'raps," said Thomas.

He hadn't told Silas and Lucy what the note said, beyond the name. This was a positive sign too. A secret kept.

"I don't see the 'arm in it," said a quiet voice. "It can be a birthday treat. This is very odd, I'll grant that, but Thomas is right. These must've been put in with . . . must've been put there for a reason."

"Feh. It isn't possible, I tell you. Suit yourselves. Go if you must, but dead is dead, and they don't speak. Anyone tells you different, they're a liar and a cheat."

Deadnettle nearly laughed as he stood to leave. Nearly. Foolish humans.

CHAPTER THREE

The Curtains Part

THEY SAID YOU WAS ALIVE? In a grave, but alive?"

"More *on* one, they said. And I'm here now, aren't I?" Thomas asked.

"Urgh. That's disgustin', that is."

Thomas wasn't so sure. The idea didn't bother him quite as much as perhaps it should have, or as much as it bothered Charley, but then, Charley hadn't grown up helping Silas from the time he could first hold a shovel. Charley hadn't really grown up anywhere much. He was just always around, sleeping in whatever corners he could find and scrounging food from any folks with some to spare. He was about Thomas's age, in as much as that was possible to guess beneath several layers of thick grime.

Thomas had found him sailing a toy boat, pieced together from scraps of wood, in the river shallows. Charley'd seen Thomas first, waving him over to ask if Thomas had any coin to spare. Never one for many words, Charley, but he'd ask that any chance he got. Thomas didn't, but coins . . . coins were on his mind, right enough. Had been since Silas and Lucy watched Thomas leave, with only a halfhearted attempt to stop him running from the house, his share of pie untouched.

He scowled down at the rippling surface. Perhaps they knew they couldn't boss him about anymore, seeing as they weren't his real parents.

"So they've got no clue where you came from?" Charley asked, flicking his boat away from the edge before it mired itself in the mud.

"Not a one. Silas just picked me up and took me home." As if Thomas had merely been another treasure surrendered from a graveyard, the very same one where they'd been digging the night before. "After a while, they named me Thomas. Said a boy needed a name, and that was that. 'Cept . . ."

"What?"

"Little while after, they had a visitor, they said." Silas hadn't wanted to tell Thomas this part; that much'd been clear as water. "Strange chap in a fine cloak who stood in the doorway and told 'em to take care of me. Gave 'em a whole sackful of silver coins and left again."

"Bet Silas spent those quick as blinking," said Charley. Thomas nodded. Silas claimed he'd gone after the man, but Thomas could only imagine how divided his attention must have been, between a purse full of money and a mysterious man who might ask for it back given half the chance.

But, again, it made no sense. The bloke had been rich, clearly, and thus there was no reason why Thomas need have grown up in two small rooms, thieving from the dead so there'd be supper on the table.

"Funny business," said Charley. The boat was stuck in a sodden clump of leaves and twigs, but he paid it no attention, deep in thought. "I reckon you should go find 'em. Your family, I mean. What I'd do, if I knew where to start, if only to tell 'em to go eat an onion for chucking me out. Maybe they had no choice. You never know. And if they's rich now, maybe they'll take you back in." Charley laughed. "And if they do, tell 'em to take me, too!"

"Right." Thomas tried to smile. He didn't have much more of an idea about where to start looking than Charley did.

But he knew one thing.

"You on a job tonight?"

Charley shook his head. "Been too few of 'em recently, to be honest. Could use a nice big haul. I'll retire like one of those fancy lords, with folks to bring me kippers and cakes on a silver tray." He lay back on the muddy earth and flung out an arm to pluck an imaginary morsel from an equally imaginary serving dish. "That'd be the life, wouldn't it, Thomas?"

It would, indeed. "If it's fancy you want, we're off to one of them grand theaters tonight," said Thomas. "Got the tickets as . . . as a present." From someone who had left Thomas a strange note. From someone who wanted him to see the performance.

But not to stay or speak to anyone. Well, he'd see about that. He'd wear a cap, though, if it mattered that much.

"Got an extra," he said to Charley. "Silas won't go."

"Sounds like a jaunt. All right, then."

He left Charley prodding at his boat with a stick again and headed for the graveyard, the tallest of the tombs and headstones poking the sky like needles up ahead.

The grave was still there. Less a grave than a patch of earth, it was true, with no marker, nowhere for mourners to kneel. A sad thought, that perhaps there was no one who *would* mourn. Perhaps this boy under a few inches of earth was the last of Thomas's own blood.

My name is Thistle, said the note in Thomas's pocket.

"Your name is Thistle," said Thomas aloud. It would have to do. There were no flowers laid down, and he didn't like to imagine what flowers might grow come summer. Young, bright things that rotted far too soon.

It seemed he couldn't stop from imagining.

Against all he had ever been taught, without shovel or spade and under the bright light of day, Thomas began to dig. The dirt stung his palms and made his fingernails so grubby he was surely in for a proper hiding from Mam— from Lucy—later, but deeper and deeper he went.

Skin, when he reached it, was colder now, the chill and the stain from the earth seeped into it. Clean enough, though, to see his own face again.

The spot on his cheek was nothing special. It wasn't in the shape of any one thing, or even very large. A tiny smudge always darker than the rest, as if Thomas never scrubbed that patch hard enough with the soap.

How odd, that this boy should have it too.

Thomas inspected Thistle's face. He really was *exactly* the same.

Overhead, the watery sun oozed down the sky toward the hills. It would frost tonight, Thomas could tell by the scent of the air. Likely the last one before summer's warmth arrived for good.

London was beautiful in frost. From this small hill,

Thomas felt as if he could see the whole city, its jumble of towns and trees and spires stitched together like an old blanket. Of course, he could only see a tiny corner, really, one frayed edge of the city spread so enormously around him.

Thomas knew well its graveyards and cemeteries, the places where folks went to be forgotten. He knew the way to the shadowy door where Silas traded the things they dug up for small coins and the way to the market where Lucy spent them. He knew the hidden crannies where food could be had for air and promises.

But beyond those, there was all of London, and beyond that, all of England and then some, of which Thomas knew nothing. Out there, somewhere—he had no inkling where beyond the first clue, the theater, but *somewhere*— were secrets. About him.

Charley was right. Thomas should find them.

"Oi! You there! What you up to?"

No voice like that ever promised good news. Without looking, Thomas scooped a few handfuls of earth and threw them to cover the face in the grave once more. Slow, limping, uneven footsteps followed as Thomas jumped up and ran across the graves to a gap in the fencing just big enough for a small, thin boy to wriggle through.

He was on the wrong side of the hill for home now, but no matter. It wasn't yet dark, and who gave a whit if night fell so completely that he couldn't see his own hand in front of his face? The whole lot of them—Silas and Lucy and whoever dumped him in that grave when he was a baby, if the story was even true—could go eat an onion. That'd make 'em cry far more than if Thomas didn't go home.

The moment of rebellion was fleeting. He wanted to go back, so's he and Lucy and Charley could go to the theater, but there was a hint of possibility in the thought of running away. He didn't have to do as Lucy and Silas bade him anymore. He didn't have to stay with them one more day if he didn't wish to. As he ventured farther from the graveyard and into a warren of narrow, cobbled streets, he was beginning to get the first hints of courage.

Children younger'n him were forever being sent away, to work down mines and up chimneys, without anyone to hold their hands or wipe their sniffles, not that Silas would ever do such things. Lucy, perhaps, but not often.

Thomas jutted his chin. Not often enough for him to miss her, to miss either of them. He'd be ab-so-lutely fine on his own. He wanted to see where he came from. He'd have an adventure, and find his family.

Silas was always telling him to find his bones. Well, he would.

And he would start tonight.

• • •

Thomas scrubbed his face and, at Lucy's insistence, scrubbed it again. No amount of effort with soap and a rag was going to get Charley completely clean, however; Lucy soon gave up on him.

"Load of nonsense, I say," said Silas from the corner, watching their preparations. "Fakes and fools, the lot of them."

Lucy turned upon him a look that would have sliced a potato clean in two. "It's very popular, I hear."

Silas scowled. "Wouldn't want to hear anything no dead folks had to say to me."

That, Thomas could well believe. He didn't expect the dead had much nice to say to Silas—or to Thomas himself. For the first time, something dark and irritable fluttered in his belly. He didn't know what they would see or hear. He didn't know why someone wanted him to see and hear it.

But they did. It was a clue, and besides, Thomas had a lifetime of doing what he was told.

Up to a point. If he were to tell Lucy that he planned to sneak away tonight and demand answers from anyone he could find involved in the performance, she'd undoubtedly forbid it.

He kept his lips firmly closed as Lucy rubbed at his cheek with her rough thumb, wet with spittle. She put a cracked mirror into his hand, and he saw the face of the boy in the grave. *My name is Thistle.*

Darkness hadn't quite fallen, but it had definitely stumbled over the horizon by the time Thomas, Charley, and Lucy closed the door on a muttering Silas and stepped out into the road.

"This is aces," said Charley, leading the way north, up into the heart of the city. "Cheers, Thomas."

Aces remained to be seen. The nervous creature in Thomas's middle flipped over once more. Lucy patted his hand.

"I'm curious too," she said. "I know as Silas never wanted to tell you, said you were ours soon as we started raising you, and that's true enough. But I tell a lie if I say I've never wondered who left you there for us, a peach for the plucking."

Thomas swallowed. They were nearing the river now, that great, black, rippling ribbon of a thing. Boats bobbed gently on the water, stark against the sky. He had no blessed clue what he would do if finding his family was as simple as skipping into the theater and announcing himself.

And he had no inkling as to why his true family would be messing about with this business, but it was no accident that the boy—Thistle—had been left right where Thomas would find him. Whoever had done so wanted him to have the tickets in Mam's little cloth bag too, put there for safe-keeping.

Every curve and groove of the cobbles pressed up

through the thin soles of Thomas's shoes as he skipped ahead to come in step with Charley, who was grinning. "Adventure!" he said. "You know, Tom, old boy, I've always figured there was more to this great wide world of ours than that as we see. Stands to reason, don't it?"

"Why d'you say that?" asked Thomas, but he had never felt alone in graveyards, and he wasn't thinking of Silas's company.

"Folks used to think fire was magic, didn't they? Then they thought clockwork was. Mebbe it is. I got my fingers on a fine old clock once, and I tell you, no matter how many times I took it to pieces and put it back together, I couldn't see what made it tick. Point is, just 'cause a thing's strange, that don't mean it's not real. Don't see why speaking to ghosts should be any different."

That was . . . a very *Charley* way of seeing the whole business, but the dark thing in Thomas's belly lightened like a sunrise. This would be fun, and he would get answers—not all of them perhaps, but some. He would find out why Thistle had been left for him. Someone there tonight would know; he could feel it clear as he could feel the paper in his pocket when he put his hand there. *Speak to no one.*

Feh, as Silas'd say.

They were almost there. A queue of people snaked

along the wall of the grand theater, and it began to slither forward as the doors were flung open. The queue was made up of people like Thomas and Lucy and Charley, dressed in their best that wasn't good enough, not compared to the ladies and gents stepping out of carriages at the curb. *They* were clothed in silks and taffetas, and they swept past the rabble straight into the theater. Such people did not do something so common as wait.

Soon, it was time to climb the marble steps. How different it felt to loose, grime-slicked cobbles.

"Stay behind me and keep close, both of you," Lucy instructed, fishing the tickets from her purse. Around her shoulder, Thomas saw a bearded man in a top hat greeting some of the fancier guests, one eye on a wooden box with a slot cut into the top. Lucy slipped the tickets inside and stepped out of the way to make room for the group behind them.

"Upstairs, quickly," she said, eyes wide at the poshness of the place. "Thomas, take your cap off; now, there's a good lad."

Their seats were in the darkest, most shadowy corner of the theater, high at the top at one end of the very last row. Far below was an ocean of jewels, and in the boxes that lined the walls too. Thomas caught Lucy staring into one of them for a long time.

"My word," she whispered, but said nothing more.

A chap in a scruffy suit stood as they neared the velvet chairs whose numbers had been printed on those fancy bits of paper. He had been seated in the one at the very end and jumped to his feet at the sight of them.

"Madam, may I help you and your sons get settled?" he asked kindly. Thomas scoffed. What kind of fool needed help sitting down? Lucy, however, nodded.

"That's very kind. Thank you, sir."

"Whitlock Jensen, spiritualist, at your service. These are yours?" He gestured to the three beside his own and, at Lucy's second nod, took her arm and led her along the row. It had been a bit of a walk from south of the river; Lucy sank into the chair with a sigh.

"Spiritualist, eh? So you know all about this, then?"

The man frowned. "I wouldn't say I know all about *this*, madam. Now, lads, you take these two." Charley hopped onto the one next to Lucy, and Thomas shook the man's hand away as he took his own. He didn't need help sitting. Standing, perhaps, after a long night of digging, when his whole body ached, but sitting never posed any difficulty.

"Oi, feel this, Tom," said Charley, running his finger across the back of the seat in front. "Ever known anything so soft?"

Thomas hadn't. Not felt anything so soft, nor seen

anywhere so packed to the brim with diamonds and gold. The walls themselves were lined with silk, and an enormous chandelier hung from the ceiling, looking like winter, so heavy it was with glittering crystals, clear and sharp as ice.

"Always puts on a show, does Mordecai," murmured the man next to Thomas. Every seat was full. The stage was hidden behind a wall of plush, mustard-colored velvet curtains. Candles flickered in their sconces.

It was proper grand, no question, but that wasn't the only thing Thomas was looking at.

There were doorways there, and there, and there. If he could lose himself in the crowd after the performance, he could slip away, find someone of whom to ask his questions. *Him.* The bearded man in the topper who had just stepped out onto the tiny lip of stage before the curtains. He might know about the boy in the grave and why Thomas had been left a note and the tickets to come here. His appearance spoke of a man who knew things, though from this distance, Thomas could make out no more than the beard, the suit, the silver-handled walking stick, and the hat, of course.

And the man opening his mouth. The theater fell silent as if a spell had been placed upon it.

"Welcome," he boomed into the utter quiet. "Welcome,

esteemed and invited guests. Such a pleasure to see you for this magnificent occasion."

Loud applause rang out. He waited for it to cease, a wide smile on his face. "Thank you. You are too kind. Now, many of you who have visited my Society know that things are done a bit differently there, but tonight, well, tonight is a time for a proper show, don't you think? So, let us begin."

"Yes, Mordecai, let's," muttered the man, Jensen, beside Thomas. "Let's see what tricks you've got in store."

He did not sound happy. Thomas spared him a glance, noted his creased brow, but Thomas's attention was drawn back to the stage as the curtains began to part. The audience gasped, though to Thomas's eye, there was nothing much to see, just a huge, polished table. It was empty, hung around the edges with more curtains of the same mustard yellow.

"Who," thundered Mordecai, "shall we invite to sit at our table? Shakespeare? A king? Cleopatra or Caesar?"

"How do we know he won't just make the whole lot up?" whispered Charley. "Even if it is possible, he could just be pretending."

They were much too far from Mordecai for him to have heard Charley, but it was as if he had.

"Perhaps," Mordecai said, "we shall start with a bit

of proof. You, there, in the second row. What an elegant dress, madam. I'm quite partial to that shade of green. Is there someone with whom you wish to speak?"

"Y-yes," said the woman. Thomas squinted, but he couldn't make her out. "M-my husband."

The dark thing squirmed in Thomas again. A tingle ran up his spine.

"Rest his soul," said Mordecai, voice dripping with sympathy. "What is his name? What is yours? And is there something, some secret the two of you share that I would have no chance of knowing?"

Whispers rippled through the theater. Thomas couldn't hear the answers she gave, but Mordecai did.

"Mr. William Harkness, late, beloved husband to Ella. Come forward, please, through the doorway that divides our worlds, and tell us how she signed her letters to you during those sad months you were forced to be apart."

Thomas's head began to ache and his teeth to chatter. Suddenly, he did not want to hear whatever endearment it was.

A voice came, from nowhere and everywhere, filling the theater. "Ella, my darling," it said, but Thomas could think of nothing but the hundreds of graves he and Silas had dug up over the years, each one containing a person who had once lived.

And who could, apparently, still speak.

So many, whose sleep he and Silas had disturbed, as they were being disturbed now.

A hot swath of nausea coursed through Thomas. His eyes rolled back in his head.

And he heard and saw nothing more.

CHAPTER FOUR

Gifts

BENEATH THE TABLE, BEHIND THE mustard curtains, Deadnettle writhed in pain. He was not alone.

Twenty-six others—all that were left—were crowded into the cage with him, locked inside as Mordecai strode free around the stage, calling out names, each older than the last.

That was simply cruel. The longer a soul had been dead, the more difficult it was to reach them. The more exhausting. The fog of effort took over Deadnettle and the rest as they focused on the names, and more as Mordecai called them out. Oh, it was wearying, even as Deadnettle knew they were being successful, his mouth open and speaking with a strange voice that joined a chorus of others. Deadnettle was barely himself as he spoke, allowing his body, his mind to be overtaken by the person speaking through him. His lips parted and his tongue moved, but these were not his words.

He liked to believe he would never say anything so silly. Some of these ancient, revered kings and queens and artists were not half as clever as people held them to be.

The roar of the audience was enormous and Deadnettle could no longer see or hear or think as he concentrated on keeping the door between the land of the living and the dead wide-open, when it is a door that likes to stay slammed shut.

Time passed. Deadnettle could not say how much, only that it was much too long before Mordecai rapped sharply on the wood and shouted, "Good night, friends!" over the clapping.

The spirits left them, vanishing like candle flames in a breeze, and Deadnettle sucked in a long breath. Every bone hurt, every muscle, and the near-silent whimpers around him told him he was not alone in his pain.

"I thank each one of you for joining our delightful supper," said Mordecai when a hush had fallen again. "Should you wish to speak to a loved one, perhaps, or ask your great-aunt Nettie where her lost ring is, do not hesitate to call upon me at the Shoreditch Spiritualist Society. I will be more than pleased to use my talents to assist you in making contact with the beyond."

His talents. Deadnettle did not miss that.

"You did well," he whispered to the others. Beside him, Marigold clung to his arm, her lips thin and white.

They'd known what to do; it was not the first time. "Take your positions, and do not shame me or you will suffer the result. And I do mean suffer," Mordecai had said, managing to smile and hiss at once. His eyes were wild, lit with madness and excitement. "I have fed you today and rested you in preparation. You will bring your greatest strengths to this greatest performance."

They had arrived at the theater in the same huge, covered cart with which he had taken them to the Society moments after the Summoning, precisely thirteen years before, to the very day.

At the time, they had been disoriented, afraid, unaware of what would be asked of them, of why they had been dragged from their homeland and brought to this horrible place.

Now Deadnettle wished for one more second of that beautiful ignorance.

Each year since, on this night, they had been brought here. And each year, on this night, but every other day as well, Deadnettle wondered to himself just how Mordecai knew of its significance.

But he would not ask. To do so would anger Mordecai. That much was certain. It would also be an admission that the date meant something of significance to Deadnettle and the other faeries. That they were stronger, more powerful now than at any other time of the year. Any admission, even of strength, was one of weakness.

He told Mordecai nothing unless he asked.

So Deadnettle clenched his long, pointed teeth and bore this travesty, as he did every other day, but magnified a thousand times by the candles and the glittering chandeliers of the theater.

When they arrived, he spoke only to repeat the words he said to them every year before climbing into the cage, while Mordecai was making his way to unlock the front doors.

"Remember," Deadnettle had said to the others, so many others, and yet so many fewer than there used to be. He always tried not to think of that, and always failed. "If we work together, combine our gifts, it will go smoothly as ever. Please Mordecai"—those words were like claws at Deadnettle's face—"and we have nothing to fear."

The younger ones, for they were all, now, younger than Deadnettle, had nodded. They hadn't been spared the vision of Mordecai's displeasure in the past, and it was an ugly sight. Mordecai might not keep iron in their home, but a lump of the stuff was never difficult to find.

"We are the gateways, never more than when the calendar reads this, the final night of the month of April. This is our most sacred night, and I know we would rather spend it elsewhere. We are altogether too far from our home. But we must do our best and take what small comfort we can from the knowledge that Mordecai could not achieve this without us. He needs us. That is *his* weakness."

It was not, however, the only one. With his excellent hearing, Deadnettle made out the thump of a walking stick and pictured the gnarled, black hand that held it. Covered by a glove in public, naturally, but Deadnettle had seen it often. Mentioning the injury was one way to raise Mordecai's ire. Deadnettle had not done so in many years, but he noticed it constantly.

On the other side of the curtains, the theater was emptying, but slowly. Naturally, everyone who had witnessed the spectacle wanted to stop and speak to the great spiritualist, or at least to shake his hand and congratulate him. It would be several more minutes at least before it was just Mordecai and the faeries, not another soul left in the whole place. Mordecai always arranged that it should be so, ushers and sweepers and ticket takers given a day's holiday. It added an air of mystery to the whole affair, which Deadnettle was certain Mordecai would have enjoyed even if there were no good reason for it, but more important, it meant that no one saw them arrive or leave.

Mordecai took great care to protect his secrets.

Or, rather, his twenty-seven secrets.

Finally, only two voices remained from what had been a crowd of hundreds in the theater.

"Deadnettle—" someone began from the other side of the cage.

"Hush!" Deadnettle said, listening to the conversation farther away.

"A fine display once again, Mordecai," said a man, just a hint of frost overlaying the warmth to his tone. "The rest of us do so wonder how you do it."

Mordecai laughed. "Hard work and a natural gift, Jensen, same as yourself. You are keeping well, I trust?"

"Well enough," said the man Jensen. "Though, clearly, not as well as yourself. Better, however, than one of your guests."

"Oh?"

"A young boy beside me was frightened to the point of fainting. Do not worry. I provided smelling salts and escorted the family out to a hansom. Paid for it too, since it was clear they hadn't the coin."

Marigold tugged on Deadnettle's arm, and he nodded. He wondered . . .

"Then I thank you for doing so without disrupting the performance," said Mordecai. It was clear that he had neither noticed the episode nor cared about it now.

"The kindness wasn't done for you."

"Now, now, Jensen, your jealousy is showing. Success has been good to me. I will not deny it. Of course," he said, and Deadnettle could just picture the wink, "it could always be better."

Behind the curtain, Deadnettle's fingers curled to fists.

"Better than to be personal spiritualist to the queen herself? Oh, yes, I spotted her, Mordecai, behind her veil in her box."

"She is a supporter of my work, indeed, and one can hardly blame her! Such a tragic tale. If I offer her some peace and solace, well, that is just a good service, don't you agree?"

"*Indeed.* Perhaps I and some of the others should come to you for lessons in . . . benevolence. You can teach us your ways, so that we might also provide such comforts to the citizens of Britain."

Mordecai laughed again, colder this time. "Oh, I think not. We must find our own path in this business, and I have found mine. Yours . . . I couldn't presume."

"You are hiding something," said Jensen, and though Deadnettle couldn't see his face, the man's rage seeped through the velvet and brushed Deadnettle's skin. "If you are doing anything to bring our good works into disrepute, I will discover it. You may have the respect of the others, but you have yet to earn mine."

"I wish you luck in that, as in all your endeavors. Good evening to you, sir," Mordecai answered mildly. Heavy footsteps stomped away, up the aisle and out the door at the back of the theater. Mordecai wandered down toward the stage, where the faeries waited, the smoke from his celebratory pipe swirling lazily up to the high, gilded ceiling.

In the small hours of the morning, Deadnettle woke Marigold, who complained, but not for long. She followed him out of the cellar and up into the street, their aching bones protesting at the climb.

"Where are we going?" she asked when they were well away from the building.

"We have several errands to run. We must check on Thomas, for I fear, as you do, that it was he who took ill last night." Jensen, the other spiritualist, hadn't sounded overly concerned, but Deadnettle was. He didn't know how much of the performance the boy had seen, and thus, how much of the truth he would understand when it was told to him.

There was nothing that could be done about it now. For the moment, Deadnettle would console himself with the fact that Mordecai obviously hadn't seen or spoken to Thomas, and that was—as Deadnettle had said in the note left in the grave—essential.

"We must give something to the boy to help him on his way," Deadnettle continued, "and we must fetch it first."

"Oh! Do we get to introduce ourselves?"

"Not quite. *You* will speak to him, but only if you promise—*promise*, Marigold—that you do not tell him who you are."

"Why not? What is the *point* of all of this, Deadnettle? I don't understand."

Deadnettle sighed and tried to think of the best way to explain it to her. The only one he could come up with sickened him to use. But these were desperate times, for him, at least.

"You have heard, in your times beneath the table, those who come to the Society but don't believe, or don't believe enough, that what is done there is truly happening?"

"Yes, of course, but—"

"But they are drawn in the first time, just a bit. And so they return, and the next time, they believe more. More the time after that, and so it goes until they tell all their friends what a gifted spiritualist Mordecai is and how everyone should visit him."

"What has this to do with Thomas?"

"We have shown him that there is something strange in his past. That there existed a boy who looked just as he does. That the people who raised him are not his true family, or not by blood. I wouldn't question the care they have given him as parents. We have shown him that speaking with the dead is possible. We are making him curious, Marigold. We are opening his mind to possibilities it would never have occurred to him to consider. We are preparing him so that when the truth comes, it is less frightening and more plausible than it would have been otherwise. And most important, we are doing it without risking ourselves, until I know he can be trusted."

"You think he'll run off and tell everyone in London about us?"

"I can't be certain he won't. Not yet. If it soothes you, today he will begin to learn what he is."

"How?"

"You will see. On Saturdays, he goes to the market with his mother. We're going to ensure he speaks to someone."

"You have been watching him."

Deadnettle nodded. Not much, but enough.

"Not yet." He did not tell her the other part of the errand, but she'd see for herself soon enough. He despised admitting even to himself that he needed her assistance, that he wasn't strong enough to do some things on his own any longer. Especially after the theater, which had sapped them all.

He led them out of Shoreditch, and every step away from the Society brought both pain and relief. Iron pressed in from every direction, where there was none in their cellar, but it soothed him to be a distance from Mordecai. In the ancient faery tongue, *captor* and *benefactor* were utterly different words, but in human English, they sounded eerily similar.

"Deadnettle?"

"Yes?"

"You heard Mordecai and that other man speaking . . ."

"I did."

"Why *don't* we go to one of the other spiritualists and tell them what Mordecai's done to us? You heard him. It doesn't sound like they'd be pleased. And if Mordecai was the one to open the gateway and bring us through to start with, maybe one of the others can open it again to send us home."

Deadnettle turned a corner. "You are a fool if you think any of them wouldn't do the same as he has done, given the chance. No human has ever given us a reason to trust them."

Her silence beside him seemed to deepen, and guilt twinged within him at her frown.

"How could they give us a reason? We have never asked one for help, Deadnettle. We hide away."

"We will never ask such a thing. Never. You are not a fool, Marigold. But even if one were good-hearted and kind, of which I have seen no evidence, I believe Mordecai to have peculiar gifts that allowed him to summon us and keep us here. I have tried to ascertain the nature of them, but I cannot. I am certain, though, that we are trapped here unless we find our own way out." And that, thought Deadnettle, meant pinning all of their hopes on Thomas.

It was tempting to give up now.

The park was empty, it being far too early for most to be awake, and those who were did not have the leisure to lounge about on dew-sodden grass instead of delivering eggs or milk or newspapers. To be safe, Deadnettle put his finger to his lips and made sure of Marigold's understanding nod before he kneeled down and prized the bottom stone out of the plinth on which a statue perched. It came free with a faint scraping noise that was overloud in the quiet dawn.

A sack of coins was wedged into the gap behind, emptier than it once was, but it hadn't been enormously full to start with. On the day, thirteen years earlier, that Mordecai had worked his human magic and dragged the faeries to England from their own land beyond the mists, none of them had been expecting it to happen. What had gone into the pouch was simply whatever the faeries had had in their pockets at the time.

Since then, they had not had chance or reason to spend much of it. Heavy silver coins with strange lettering around the edges tended to attract all manner of unwanted attention.

Well, spending was a risk Thomas would have to take. Another test. Deadnettle counted out several, polished one on his cloak, and held it up to the curious light caused by the meeting of the fading moon and the growing sun.

Wintercress. Her sharp, beautiful profile glittered. To look at her was to know that she was special, the faery queen. Deadnettle touched her forehead, then nearly dropped the coin as he felt Marigold's eyes on him. Quickly, he put the pouch and the stone back in place and stood, composing himself for their next tasks.

Their journey across the river took them within hearing distance—which was still quite far for a faery—of Thomas's home. Deadnettle stood, listening, until he could be certain of two things: that the boy was awake and speaking with his mother over his breakfast, and that he would indeed accompany her to the market.

They stopped next at the graveyard gates.

They crossed the river in silence that lasted until Marigold stopped him at the graveyard gates. "Let me," she said, and as with the last time they were in this place, he let her even though he shouldn't have. She grasped the iron, and muffled her scream as the new angry brand lay itself over the healing one.

"It didn't hurt much," she assured him. He had no choice but to believe her.

The soil had been softened by their digging, and Thomas's, and so it was quick work to pull Thistle from the earth and replace him with the coins Deadnettle put into another small pouch. He saw the moment comprehension broke across her small face as to why they were not just leaving her friend buried, but she did not mention it until they were almost back at the river again. Panting, they laid the body down, wrapped in its musty cloak, on the muddy bank.

"It's been hurting you," she said, and there was no hint of question in her voice. But she did not look at him, instead busying herself with finding heavy enough rocks with which to weigh Thistle down.

"Yes," he agreed. "And this is not the time for me—for any of us—to be weaker than we absolutely must. Humans"—he spat into the water—"and their cruel, silly faery stories. Painting us as cunning, conniving, sneaky creatures, when nothing could be further from the truth. Any lie we tell hurts us, even when told to a thieving monster such as Mordecai."

By herself, in a burst of strength, Marigold pushed Thistle's body into the dark, black waters. "There," she said, calm as the river itself. "Now it won't be a lie. We've done with him what we do with everyone who leaves." Her face twisted suddenly into disgust. "Mordecai should do this himself," she spat. "But he would have to touch us then, wouldn't he?"

"Yes," Deadnettle whispered. The relief was immediate, the burden lifted from him as surely as the stones were dragging Thistle to the bottom to join the others, where no one would ever find them. Peace, for them at least, but some for Deadnettle, too. Already he ached less, and his muscles felt stronger, despite the long and taxing night. "Thank you."

"Why do they tell such stories about us?"

It was *nearly* irritating, Marigold's almost ceaseless talent for asking questions to which he had no good answers, or none of which he could be certain, but instead a sadness lapped at him like the water at their feet. "I suppose because it would have been difficult to make us sound evil, back in the time when our land and this one were one and the same. Lies are reflections; in this case, a mirror was held to the truth so its exact opposite was told."

Marigold nodded and looked up at the lightening sky. "Where are we going now?"

Filled with more energy, lighter on his feet, Deadnettle took Marigold's hand and led her to the market. She seemed suddenly weary, but it had been an exhausting time for her, too. Mordecai wouldn't be looking for them until afternoon, the fancy ladies who visited the Society preferring to drink tea in bed until at least midday, or whatever it was that such women did.

It wasn't difficult to locate what, or rather whom, Deadnettle required next. Mordecai and his fellow spiritualists were at the forefront of the craze that swept the country for contacting loved ones who had already crossed to the beyond. Indeed, it could be said that Mordecai was leading and the others scrapped at his ankles like terriers, but the fad had created people who catered to every aspect of the Mysteries.

Whether anyone but Mordecai actually succeeded in efforts to contact the dead, or see into the future, or anything else these people claimed to do, was a different question, but said people were certainly easy enough to find. Especially in the poorer areas of the city, and those were everywhere. He instructed Marigold to wait outside for him and knocked on the door. Curtains twitched at the window, a face appearing over the notice advertising her gifts—dubious though they certainly were—as a clairvoyant. Deadnettle doubted she did much custom at home, but she wouldn't turn anyone away. Locks slid. She looked precisely as such a person might be expected to, dark haired and plump and lips stained with carmine, and Deadnettle doubted she could see beyond the present hour—or was bright enough to remember the past, come to that.

Perfect.

"You going to give me a good reason why I should move my pitch?" she demanded, when he explained what she was to do. "Never been to that market in my life. No one down there interested in tomorrow. They know it'll be the same as today, the same grubbing about to make a living."

Deadnettle withdrew two large silver coins from the pocket of his cloak. "These are good reasons. Do you need better ones?"

Her eyes widened. She shook her head.

"I thought not. Where is your sign?"

It was a crude thing, cheap wood and flaking paint, but

no matter. The woman opened her mouth when Deadnettle dipped his finger into the same bottle of midnight-blue ink with which he had first written to Thomas and began to stain the wood with words she could not read, but she remained silent, hushed by the weight of the silver.

"The boy will come to you," Deadnettle said. "You will know him when you see him."

He told her what to say.

CHAPTER FIVE

Pasts and Futures

THOMAS PUT DOWN HIS BOOK. It wasn't fair, really, Mam expecting him to do his lessons this morning. He'd been ill at the theater, and Mam had put him to bed as soon as they'd arrived home. Charley had jumped out soon as they'd crossed the river and scampered off to where he was sleeping this week, ratty with the driver for not letting him have a turn at the reins.

That had been exciting, riding in a posh hansom. Almost worth swooning in the first place, only not, because he'd lost any chance he had for sneaking off to speak to Mordecai. Much as he'd protested that he was perfectly fine, soon as he'd been carried outside to take the air, Mam wouldn't hear of going back inside to see the rest of the performance. She'd argued with the man, too, the one who'd helped them into their seats and then helped them outside, when he insisted on paying for the carriage, but— and this was the most shocking bit of unfairness—eventually she'd let *him* have his way.

He yawned, and Lucy glanced sharply at him. "I reckon you need a mite more sleep," she said, but Thomas shook his head. He had woken very early, while it was yet dark, and though Thomas was quite used to being awake in the small hours, he wasn't accustomed to seeing them from the direction of the morning, as it were. A strange dream echoed for the instant after he opened his eyes, and then it faded away.

A voice, calling out in the night, calling to him. He could guess only too well where such a thought had come to him, and he shivered.

It wasn't right, disturbing the dead like that. Couldn't be right. And, somehow, his real family were tangled up in it.

A muffled *thump* came from the other room, and Silas emerged, bleary, scratching at his whiskers. He splashed water on his face from the jug and bowl in the corner before blinking at Thomas and Lucy.

"Back to yerself this morning?" he asked. "Good. I told ye it was silliness to go. Keep your strength up today. Holiday's over. We'll be out with the shovels again tonight."

The dark thing inside Thomas flicked a lazy arm. No. He couldn't. Not now. Not after the voice in the theater and with the memory of the last grave he'd dug up.

"I ain't going."

Silas's mouth opened and closed, but no words came out.

Neither could remember the last time Thomas had defied him, bold as brass like that.

"May I ask why not?" Silas asked finally. There was an odd tone to his voice, almost mocking, but that wasn't precisely it, and it quickly went away. "Look, lad, I know you saw an awful thing. It's been an odd few days, right enough. Best thing to do is get back to work. You won't feel no better with an empty belly, and this is how we put food on the table."

"And we won't starve if we leave off one more night," said Lucy. "Let 'im rest, Silas."

"Fine," muttered Silas. A moment later, the door slammed. Thomas's shovel rattled on its nail on the wall. Lucy wiped her hands on a rag that only served to make them dirtier and sighed.

"How are you feeling, poppet?"

She had not called him *poppet* in longer than it'd been since he'd refused to do whatever Silas asked. And Thomas knew that he couldn't answer her, not honestly, because he wasn't certain himself. It had been, as Silas'd said, an odd few days.

Strange wasn't the half of it, really.

"Do you truly not know where I come from?" he asked. The lines on her face seemed to deepen, but possibly that was a trick of the firelight, which could turn shadows to ghosts and flames to staring, screaming faces.

"We don't." Lucy sighed again, and it was just now occurring to Thomas how easily he'd stopped thinking of them as Mam and Papa. As if part of him had always known that the reflection in the mirror glass—and now the face in the grave—looked nothing like either one, or even a mixture of the two. "I always fancied the man who visited sounded like 'e was from the south somewhere, but that don't mean nothing these days. And he spoke that quiet, I couldn't be sure regardless."

South. It wasn't a great help, even if it were true and not a flight of fancy—or an outright untruth. But it was something, perhaps.

South could mean a great many places, names Thomas had only heard or spelled out with his finger on torn maps. Brighton, Torquay, Glastonbury. Strange people with their strange accents brought from those streets to the lanes of London, words sometimes so thick and garbled Thomas could hardly understand them.

The same feeling that had come over him the last time he'd been in the graveyard came again now, of the sheer vastness that lay all around, and that it was hiding something.

"May I go find Charley? I'll be back 'fore we go to the market."

Charley'd likely be up near the river, and the river, why, that was almost in Shoreditch, and that's what the bearded, toppered man had said the previous night, wasn't it? The Shoreditch Spiritual Society.

Lucy whirled to fix Thomas with a stare that fixed him in place sure as a nail would. "Not today. This is your home, Thomas. Silas and I are your family. We's the ones who wanted you. I might not've been raised with much, and we might not as have much to give you, but I was brought up to believe that means something, and you'd best believe it too."

"Yes'm," Thomas whispered. Guilt ran up his back like a thousand of the spiders that shared his blankets. Shoreditch would have to wait.

"Good lad. But if you're desperate to be outside these walls, can't say's I blame you. Let's head off now. Wrap up warm, and we'll go see if we can get the butcher to give us a piece of stew meat without asking an arm and a leg in return."

After finding Thistle in the grave, the note written in its bizarre, spiky letters, the tickets, and the séance, Thomas wondered if the fact that there were still things as boring as mutton to be thought of wasn't perhaps the strangest part of this whole business.

There wasn't, in fact, much need to wrap up at all. A warm sun shone on the soot and muck in the gutters outside, making even the filth seem bright and new and pleasant. Inside his pocket, Thomas kept his hand wrapped around the coins he'd fetched from his box so they wouldn't jangle.

They weren't worth an arm and a leg, but he didn't want to give them to Lucy or the butcher.

He needed them. It was possible that whoever had left the note and the tickets had truly wished for Thomas to speak to Thistle at the theater, and the answers were farther afield than Shoreditch. Brighton, Torquay, Glastonbury. He would need the coins to get there.

If he could sneak away.

It took an absolute age for them to reach the market, or it felt so. Lucy kept stopping to greet people, and Thomas was forced to do the same so nobody would think him rude, especially not Lucy. He needed her in a kindly mood when they finally reached the square crammed with ramshackle stalls and bright, frayed bits of bunting. He smiled at the mother of the Robinson girls and an old man with a walking stick and a young chap whose mongrel wove in and out between Thomas's ankles.

A few feet at a time, they edged closer to the market, until Thomas could hear the shouts of the stall holders, each trying to tempt customers to buy from them and not from the thieving swine across the way.

It made Thomas smile. They were thieving swine, of course. Every last one of 'em.

So was he, when it came down to it, thanks to Silas. But not anymore.

"Be a love," Lucy said. "Take this and go fetch us an onion." She waved a package of meat wrapped in cheap newspaper in the direction of a farmer's table, the vegetables wilted and brown. With her other hand, she slipped a penny into Thomas's palm.

Someone tapped on his shoulder. Thomas turned and faced a pretty girl in a worn, mud-colored cloak. She gave him the oddest stare Thomas had ever been on the pointy end of, but that was girls for you. The Robinson twins were always giving him funny looks too.

"Hello," she said. Her voice wasn't quite as strange as her expression, but there was something a bit off about it.

"Hullo," said Thomas, there being no reason to be rude.

"Are you lost, child?" Lucy asked.

"Oh, no," said the girl. "It's only that my . . . my uncle gave me a coin to get an ice, but I've looked, and they're so big, I'd never finish one myself. I've no one to share it with, so I've been waiting until I saw someone who might like to."

The ices. Thomas wanted to see them every time he made this outing with Lucy. They couldn't buy one, of course, but he could look while his mouth watered at how he imagined they would taste, as bright on his tongue as their colors were. Cherry red and blackberry purple.

"Well, that's right kind of you," said Lucy. "You sure you was given that coin to spend on sweets?"

"Oh, yes."

"May I? Please?" Thomas asked.

"Oh, I daresay you may. Hurry back, mind, and bring the onion with you."

The girl put her hand inside Thomas's, comfortable as if they were the best of friends, and pulled him into the crowd.

"What's your name?" he asked her. "Seeing as we'll be sharing an ice, feels only proper to know."

She smiled at him. "Mari—Mary."

"Quite contrary?"

She looked puzzled. "Pardon me?"

"You know," Thomas urged, "the rhyme. *Mary, Mary,*

quite contrary . . ." In fact, he himself couldn't remember the rest.

"Oh," said Mary. "Yes. I mean, no. Just Mary." She scowled a bit, but quickly turned her mouth upward again.

The ices were on the other side of the bustling square. The cobblestones underfoot ran slick with stinking stuff that could no longer be called water, though it had leaked from the fishmonger's big barrels of thrashing creatures. Jostled and bumped, Thomas and Mary fought their way through to the stall, where the ices sat glowing brighter than the jewels in the theater.

Surely tasted better too. True to her word, Mary bought a large one and led him to a sheltered spot between a baker's and a stall hung the whole way around with golden spangles. He didn't have time to look at what it sold, but he knew it hadn't ever been there before and decided to look when they were done, for Mary was already enjoying the ice, and she *had* offered him half.

Thomas'd never eaten anything so good. The flavor burst like fireworks on his tongue, sweet and sour all at once in the way the best summer raspberries were.

No sooner had Mary swallowed her last mouthful than she dropped the now-empty twist of paper at their feet and gave him another odd stare. "I must go!" she said. "Isn't all that gold pretty? I just noticed. Thank you, Thomas!"

"But—"

But she was gone, dashed off and swallowed by the crowd. Perhaps Thomas was now *attracting* strangeness, and this sort was certainly more pleasant than graves or ghostly voices.

He stepped out of their spot, peering around for a grocer's, remembering the onion, and then turned to look at the sign in front of the glittery new stall.

He spun, squinting through the crowd for any glimpse of the girl. She had called him Thomas, though now he thought on it, she hadn't asked his name.

She was gone, and only the stickiness on Thomas's lips assured him she had been real in the first place.

The sign was real.

Charlatans, Silas always spat about such people. Liars and fakes, dishonest souls out to rob a man of his last copper, which was a bit rich from a man who stole what little the dead had left.

Thomas didn't know if it was usual for them to be out in the open like this, with a sign proudly proclaiming it, but all sorts ended up in and around the market, trying to scrape by a living. It wasn't just meat and vegetables.

FORTUNE-TELLER, read the sign. And under that . . .

Under that were those same strange letters as were on the note in his pocket, the ones it made his head ache to read.

COME IN, they said.

Inside, a funny smell stung Thomas's nostrils. Something foreign and strange, wafting from the shadows.

Inside, it was painted with shadows.

"Hello," said a voice.

A candle burst to life.

If forced to close his eyes and imagine such a person, Thomas would have described a fortune-teller who appeared exactly as this one did. Plump, with long eyelashes and bright red lips, surely the result of carmine, which Thomas knew of only because Silas had once given Lucy some as a present. Her thick hair was jet-black where it wasn't streaked with white as pale as milk. Everywhere, she glittered with enough gold to make Silas reconsider robbing only from the dead.

"A young one. A long future." She smiled. "And what is your name, young one?"

Thomas rather thought she should already know, but he hadn't paid her yet, which might explain it. "Thomas," he said. He wondered if he'd had a different name before, whether someone had wished him good-bye with it as they put him in the grave as a babe. "Where do those letters come from, the ones on the sign? I need to know."

"Thomas." Her voice was as rich as the red on her lips. "Do you have money?"

Silas could be right about them. Charlatans, swindlers. But Thomas withdrew his hand from his pocket, a handful of coins clattering on the table at which she sat. She considered him for a moment and selected two of the smallest. Her face paled beneath its paint. "Where did you get these?" she demanded.

"Someone gave 'em to me." Which was strictly true. Silas had.

"No one living," she muttered, then seemed to decide any coin was better than none, even one taken from the eyes of the dead. "Sit," she ordered, pointing a ringed finger at a worn velvet stool by his knees.

Her hand, when it wrapped around his, was soft, powdery as a butterfly's wing, and it flew away just as quickly to rest on her heart.

"Not a young one," she gasped, black eyes wide. "An *old* one." Trembling, she reached across to hold his cheeks hard enough to hurt as she stared into his eyes. "Old and *broken!*"

Thomas tried to speak, but he could make only a muffled sound.

"So broken!" the fortune-teller shrieked. "Old one, *what happened to you?*"

CHAPTER SIX

A Fistful of Silver

THREE STREETS AWAY, THE POWDER from the fortune-teller's hands was still on his cheeks, cool against his heated skin. Her last words screamed around his head.

Go back to the grave, old one! Go back to the grave!

After that, she had said no more, had only stared at Thomas with blazing terror in her eyes, the fear burning into him through her fingertips until he wrenched himself free and ran. And ran.

Old? Broken? He was perfectly young and healthy, thank you very much, and she was a fraud, just as Silas said about those people. Hadn't even let him tell her what he needed to know before she put on a performance worthy of one of those big fancy stages up in the middle of the city. A big fancy stage like he'd seen last evening.

Giving him his money's worth, wasn't she?

Not hardly. Thomas's stomach sank. He'd left every one of his coins on her rickety table—so that was her game. Get the mug to empty his pockets, then scare the daylights out of 'im. He felt inside his pockets, just in case, but he had nothing left, not even the penny Lucy had given him for the onion, and she'd be looking for at least a halfpenny to come back with it.

And him. She'd be looking for him by now.

But he *couldn't* be a mug. He'd seen those letters on her sign, hadn't he? And he'd seen the sign because he'd been standing right there, eating raspberry ice.

With a girl who had appeared from nowhere, and returned there.

He needed to find her again. He could not go back to Silas and Lucy. He hadn't been *planning* to, though now that he thought on it, none of his plans had worked out altogether very well. If he was going to find his family, Thomas was going to have to get a great deal better at plans, and quickly.

There'd never been much need for him to plan anything. He had always done as Silas and Lucy bade him, and that filled all the hours he was awake. Thomas was never certain whether that was because he was a good boy, or because he had learned young indeed what happened if he did not: sent to bed without supper, or forced to scrub every last speck of dirt from the floor. Didn't much matter either way, he supposed.

But he did know someone who'd always looked after himself, who knew the city where living people dwelled, not just dead ones.

Thomas would find Charley—

"Thomas! Get here, this instant!"

Another plan scuppered. Thomas turned toward Lucy and watched her face shift rapidly from blotchy red anger to something much more gentle.

"Thomas, what's happened? Have you taken ill again? You look a proper state." She strode up to him and took his hand. "I think you've had too much excitement these few days. It's not good for the humors. Come, poppet. Let's go home."

Let her think he was ill. Then he could think without her pestering him to talk or do his lessons, or about the onion. Indeed, she did none of those things on the way back to the little house or while she tucked him into his bed. Silas hadn't returned from wherever he'd gone. Thomas knew better than to ask where, even if he'd wished to, and when Silas returned just in time for supper to be put on the table, Thomas pretended to sleep.

He had to roll over to hide his slight, unwilling smile at Silas's complaint that the stew was very bland.

At some point during his busy show of being asleep, Thomas actually did drift off, head filling with jagged dreams of hands on his face, then two pairs of hands on two faces exactly the same. *Old ones, old ones, old ones,* screamed the fortune-teller's rich voice.

When he opened his eyes, the room was empty and Silas's boots were gone from beside the door. So was his shovel. It was late, then. As the days grew longer, Silas— and usually Thomas as well—waited an extra few minutes every evening for night to fully fall, for the darkness to cover their wicked deeds in whatever graveyard had been chosen that day.

One of Lucy's soft snores rattled from the other room.

Thomas wasn't going to get a better chance and, beneath the curiosity and oddness of the past days, he was simply fed up. He was going to find out what was happening and who was behind all of this.

For a brief moment, he wished to be back in the few minutes before he had chosen that fresh, unmarked plot of earth, just so as he could turn away from it and choose a different grave. He would have come home with Silas, hopefully a few trinkets richer, and still thought of them as Mam and Papa. He wouldn't see a face like his own each time he shut his eyes, as if they were lined inside with mirror glass.

But it was far, far too late for that now, and everything that had happened since had put his thoughts through one of them fancy mangles he sometimes saw in shop windows as he and Silas crept to work and home again.

No, Thomas could not go back to the way things had been, but he could go back to the spot on which he had stood two nights previous.

Go back to the grave, old one.

There wasn't much hope it would give him any blasted idea what to do next, but it was something. It would get him out of this room that no longer felt like home. Silas wouldn't be there; he always left at least a fortnight before returning to any given one, enough time for caretakers and policemen to get tired of waiting for the thief to return, what with so many other crimes to occupy the latter and exhaustion to overwhelm the former.

It worked, because they had never been caught. The previous day was the closest Thomas'd ever come.

Surely the body would be gone, thanks to the caretaker who had chased him off and most certainly discovered the disturbed grave that was never meant to be there to begin with. Surely Thomas wouldn't have to go near it, dragged there by the temptation to gaze upon it just one more time.

A cracked, faded satchel sat in the corner, cast there by Silas when he'd found a better one, in the way Silas *found* anything. Quiet as he could, Thomas packed every last scrap of clothing he owned, and Lucy's spare shawl besides.

The door creaked. They always do, just when a person's trying to be quiet as a breath.

The graveyard gates were cold iron in his hand, the metal sucking the last of the chill from the air. They were locked, but it had been many years since such a problem had stood in Thomas's way. Getting into graveyards had almost been the first thing Silas taught him—for, as Silas had rightly said at the time, without that, there wasn't much point in teaching Thomas anything else.

Moonlight turned small white stones to glowing paths. Thomas didn't need to watch where he was going. He knew, and all was silent. No one would disturb him now.

A branch creaked.

Rats skittered, kicking the pebbles.

"Hello?" Thomas whispered, for one could never be too careful. Only the wind whispered back, rustling its greeting through the brand-new leaves on the trees overhead.

Perhaps there were ghosts. Thomas never felt alone in graveyards, and this night he felt more imagined eyes on him than ever. They prickled the hairs on the back of his neck and turned his breath shallow.

There he was, right where he'd first spotted the easy pickings that'd turned out to be anything but. Thomas could picture Silas nearby.

Find your bones, the trees whispered in Silas's voice.

But, as Thomas had guessed, his bones were gone. The shallow grave had been emptied, but it was not yet refilled with the pile of earth that sat beside it. He could only wonder what the caretaker had thought, discovering it. Likely the police had been called in, though perhaps not. One less urchin on the street, one less mouth to feed, might be nothing for anyone to worry about.

Perhaps only Thomas wanted to know the truth.

He inched toward the uneven hole, slowly, slowly. No, there was no boy in there, looking like Thomas or anyone else.

There was *something*, however. He climbed down and picked it up, surprised at its weight, unsurprised by the gentle clinking noise that came from within.

"Hello?" Thomas called, too loud to be careful, just in case whoever had left the bag had stayed to watch him collect it.

That was real silver, that clink. None of the shoddy stuff.

Only the trees replied, but Thomas was certain.

Someone was watching him.

Someone was *helping* him.

• • •

Why, he could buy a palace with this. The coins glittered in the light, like a handful of stars. Two handfuls. Three. He let all but one slide back into the leather pouch and held the last between his fingers. It was strange, the face etched on one side utterly unfamiliar, and he'd no hope of identifying what was on the other. Thomas had never been much good with plants and herbs.

The markings around the edges . . . those, he knew. He saw them when he closed his eyes, etched not on silver but on paper and wood.

Queen Wintercress, Thomas read as the letters wriggled and his eyes watered.

The trees shivered, and so did Thomas.

Something very odd indeed was going on. His head swam with what he had seen and heard since the first time he'd stood right here.

Climbing from the grave for the very last time—any grave, of this he was resolved—Thomas peered around, slowly at first, then darting his head back and forth, trying to catch glimpses from the corners of his eyes of anyone who didn't want to be seen.

There was no one there, but Thomas was coming to believe that didn't mean they *weren't* there. To be safe, he crept around the graveyard, even down into the dark, old bit where the moonlight didn't shine and the gravestones had crumbled to dust along with the people they named.

No one.

A thought struck, and he tucked the pouch inside his satchel, with Lucy's scarf wrapped twice around it. Any London rake worth his salt would have Thomas by the throat at the first *clink*. He let himself out the same way he'd come, turning his little metal tools in the lock until it snapped closed. Shadowy figures moved around the night as he walked home, none paying the slightest bit of mind to Thomas, their business as dark and nefarious as his own, at least.

Thomas's stomach growled. His hand fished in the satchel and closed around the sack of silver. Oh, the things he could eat now! Strawberry tarts and jellied eels and a whole pie if he liked, dripping with gravy.

A bundle of rags woke when nudged with Thomas's toe, and a grubby hand seized his ankle.

"I'll 'ave your guts for—oh, it's you. Whatcha doing waking me up for?"

"Need your help. There's breakfast in it if you do."

That got Charley up jackrabbit-quick. "What can I do for you, my lad?"

Thomas checked over both shoulders, twice, before showing Charley one of the coins. "Someone left these for me. Think the same folks as buried my brother, in the same place. Need to sell 'em for something that won't get me nicked for spending."

"Too right," said Charley, who'd spent more than one night with a bruised ear from a copper sure he'd thieved the coins in his pockets. Of course, Charley usually had. "Look foreign. Wonder what it says. I know just where to go. Used to be a friend of Silas's."

Such places were never officially open, and thus, they never closed.

"No beggars!" snarled the toothless, straggly man who answered at first sight of Thomas and Charley. "Got nuffink here for your ilk. Get away."

"What'll you give me for this?" Thomas asked, drawing out one of the coins as the door painfully hit the side of his foot. *That* got the chap's attention, though he tried not to show it, eyes widening, shoulders shrugging in a disinterested sort of way. His fingers betrayed more interest, darting up to grip the edge with long yellow fingernails.

Thomas held fast. "Try to take it, and I'll set Silas on you. He's pretty good at digging graves, if you'll recall." It was an empty threat; Thomas wouldn't tell Silas they'd come here, and far as he knew, Silas'd never killed more than a fish for supper, but the chap likely didn't know that. There were rules down here about thieving from your own.

"Hmmm. Prob'ly tin in the middle. No good even melted down. Maybe worth a guinea."

"It's real," said Charley. Thomas nodded. The coin was worth at least five times that, or more. "Four quid. We'd melt it down ourselves, get even more, but we're in a hurry."

"Two."

"Three." Charley's eyes glittered.

Now Thomas knew how the people in the graves felt, robbed almost blind.

"Two, or I'll shout for a copper to ask where you got your grubby 'ands on it."

"Three," said Charley, "or *I'll* shout for one and tell him to have a proper good look 'round your house."

"Hmph. Stay there."

Thomas smiled at the man's back as it disappeared down the corridor. "Good one, mate." Charley grinned, a job well done.

Two greasy pounds went into Thomas's pocket, well away from the silver, and one disappeared into Charley's palm. It was a great deal more than the promised breakfast, but Charley'd earned it, and what was left would do Thomas a nice while, no matter how many pies he ate. They got the breakfast, too, a dozen sizzling sausages that dripped oil on their fingers and which had cost far too much, but every bite was worth it. When he needed to, he'd sell another of the strange coins. Whoever had left them for him must have known Thomas couldn't waltz into a shop, bold as brass, and plunk down a coin worth that much.

They were foreign, to be sure, but from where, he didn't know. He had a feeling who would, however. Someone who could sense where a coin had been just by touching it. Would she shriek *old one* the instant she saw him?

"Charley," said Thomas, chewing. "Who are the *old ones*?"

"How d'you mean?"

"I don't know. It was something—something I heard a man say at the market." There, that was safe enough.

"We-ell," said Charley, "there's some as call the faery folk that, don't they? In the old stories? Me mam used to tell 'em to me, 'fore she died."

"Do they?" Thomas'd had a book of faery stories once, but he couldn't recall it much.

"Hmmm." Charley bit off half a sausage and swallowed it in one go. "And you know as I believe in that stuff, but I say there's too many tales, strange creatures living in the hills and causing mischief, and don't none of the stories agree with each other. Some say they're kind, gentle creatures, with great magic powers for healing and whatnot.

Like doctors, but without the leeches, you know. Others say they do dark magic and lie to humans or steal from them. Some say they steal babies from their cots, leaving faery children, changelings, behind in their place. You'd think if there was any truth to it, more people would get it right. Or at least agree on some of 'em."

Indeed, you'd think so, thought Thomas, but he didn't say it aloud.

Faery folk. Old ones.

Broken.

It couldn't be.

"Do they look like regular people?"

"Some think so. Gracious, what an 'orrid thought, that they could be walking around with us folk never knowing."

The street blurred in front of Thomas's eyes.

He shook his head. If it'd been a show he was after, he perhaps hadn't paid the fortune-teller enough, even with leaving her every last coin he had.

"You look white as a ghost, Tom."

Lots of people believed in ghosts. Thought they haunted graveyards and houses, unable to rest, forever. Why couldn't they exist? Thomas never felt alone in graveyards, always watched, always heard. And if they could, then . . .

Dawn was beginning to pinken the sky. Another hour or

two and the market would be setting up. Secretive dealers in stolen goods weren't the only people who never closed up shop. Charley declined to join him, wishing to run off instead to spend his newfound riches on who-knew-what. Likely better not to ask.

"Do something for me, would you?" Thomas felt inside his satchel, drew out two more of the coins, and held them in front of Charley's wide eyes. "Give these to Lucy and Silas for me. Tell them . . . Tell 'em I'll be back soon as I can."

Two coins, because that was what Silas always let him keep from the graves. Charley took them, nodding. He knew the rules too. The coins would make it to Lucy's purse or Silas's grubby fist. Charley skipped away. Thomas walked slowly until an aproned woman stopped him.

"Hungry, lad? Look as if you could use a square meal or four."

He still was, even after all the sausages.

Thomas chewed his fifth piece of bacon, elbows on an oily slick countertop, happily aware there was no Lucy to tell him to mind his manners. As if there'd ever been anyone to impress at supper. She'd always made him behave as if the queen, bored of Whitstable oysters on fine china, was coming down to slurp a bowl of watery stew.

"'Nother egg, please," said Thomas, sliding payment

across the slick counter before the jolly woman in her stained apron could ask for it.

He ate that one, and another after it.

A great tiredness began to over take him, but there was no time to sleep or place to do it. Soon enough, he'd find somewhere. Could go and stay in the poshest hotel in all of London if he liked.

The first shouts of *Finest spuds, won't find cheaper!* were filtering from the market. Thomas slid from his chair and looped the satchel across his body, ready to hold tight as he crossed the square to the golden curtain that beckoned like the sun.

Early though the hour was, the market was already crowded with housewives and pickpockets, charwomen and children. They blocked his way as they bent to look at carrots or pocket watches, but Thomas slipped around them, eyes peeled for the golden flash of brightness.

It wasn't there.

It wasn't anywhere.

"'Scuse me," Thomas shouted, pushing his way through a gaggle of chattering women and around a very portly man smoking a pipe to a stall piled with ancient, motheaten rugs. "Was there a fortune-teller here yesterday?"

"Search me." The stall keeper slapped his hand down, then coughed as a cloud of dust from one of his rugs billowed up into his face.

Thomas walked around the market twice, and a third time for luck, but none came his way. She was gone. Clenching fingers and teeth, he pushed his way from the mass and ran from the square for the second time, just as confused as the first.

Angry, too. A great red anger bubbled up inside him. Was someone *trying* to completely do his head in?

Nothing made any blasted *sense* anymore.

He took a deep breath.

"I know you're watching," he said, quiet and firm. "You were watching in the graveyard. You've been watching me. I think you're trying to tell me something, but blowed if I know what. Please tell me. I must know. Tell me what to do next."

There was no answer. Here, in the midst of the crumbling buildings, there weren't even any trees to whisper.

A single scrap of paper fluttered down from the sky, a snowflake in springtime.

On it, in the strange letters that were becoming all too familiar, was a time and a place. Tonight.

CHAPTER SEVEN

The Shoreditch Spiritual Society

D EADNETTLE WATCHED THE PIECE OF paper
flutter slowly down, shifting the winds so it
would land exactly where he wished it to. These
days, that much tested the very limits of his magic.

But land it did, right in young Thomas's hand. That the
boy would obey the instruction, Deadnettle had no doubt.
Everything he had seen thus far gave him hope of this at
least, and hope, in this dark time, was a precious thing
indeed.

He had no fear that the boy would look up and see him,
for Deadnettle was miles away, atop one of London's many
spiky towers. Until now, Deadnettle had chosen to follow
the boy closely, but now he resisted the need to be near the

last of Wintercress's blood. He would see the boy tonight, and so he did only what he must in order to know where Thomas was, using his inhuman gifts. In the faery realm, the astonishing senses—eyesight and the like—that they were blessed with were a wondrous gift, but not here. No, here Deadnettle wished to be blind and deaf and to not feel a thing when iron accidentally brushed his skin.

He cautiously skirted some now, an old bit of railing, and slid down a drainpipe. He would return to the Society to wait for nightfall, the time marked by bells every quarter of an hour. Why must this cursed city have so many bells? Every chime sent fire through his rattling bones, an agony like lightning striking in his head. The sound was much softer in the cellar, but even Mordecai, with his magic and *benevolence*, could not silence them.

Iron and bells. They were not the only traps with which Mordecai kept the faeries captive, but they were incredibly effective at ensuring the faeries had no energy with which to fight back.

When darkness fell, Deadnettle ascended to the street, the hood of his heavy cloak pulled around his face. Brown was best, or blue; hysterical ladies tended to scream or faint at the sight of a figure dressed head to toe in black. Deadnettle was not the specter of death they imagined, but it was a terrifyingly close guess, and showing his face to explain anything would raise a number of inconvenient questions. Thin skin and razor-sharp bones beneath might be explained as illness, but the brightly colored eyes, with neither white nor pupil, were particularly an issue. The time was long past that he had the strength to make himself appear human for a few minutes, though he had once been one of the most adept at it, had practiced it as a party trick back home.

Horses and carriages—some garishly opulent, others barely held together with prayers and rusted nails—passed by, splattering muck as the beasts attempted to put as much space between themselves and Deadnettle as possible and the drivers whipped their flanks. Animals were so much more adept at sensing the *other*. In deference, Deadnettle kept as close to the railing as he could without searing pain, but it was never enough.

He had no sympathy for the passengers, but the horses were as enslaved as he, bound by metal and leather.

Slowly, he walked toward the building that was his prison, though outwardly it was very pleasant. Red brick and white window sashes, stretching the width between two streets. A small plaque beside the tall front doors advertised the business conducted there, but this caused no alarm from passersby. Why, there were three other spiritualists over in Covent Garden alone, two more in

Fitzrovia, including the one named Jensen, with whom Mordecai had argued at the grand performance. Not to mention an enormous number of hacks or charlatans with bits of handwritten card propped up against the windows of dingy rooms facing the street, like the fortune-teller he had found to deliver his message to Thomas.

Some might question why this one was so much nicer than any of the others, larger and reeking of wealth. Some might not. Other spiritualists did, for certain. Jensen was not the only one. But they had never come close to discovering Mordecai's method.

The desire to seek counsel with the dead had gripped Britain as a fever; for those doing the seeking, it didn't do to be overly curious about how such things were achieved.

The plaque was ringed in iron—to mock them, Deadnettle thought. In fairness, and it was quite a challenge to be fair, it was the only piece of metal in the entire place.

THE SHOREDITCH SPIRITUAL SOCIETY

Ha. A Spiritualist. A liar, more like. A warlock, a sorcerer, an evil soul, showing an acceptable face to the citizens of London.

Two well-heeled ladies were emerging. Deadnettle pressed himself into the shadows, unnecessary though it was, for they were not paying him the slightest bit of attention. Eyes bright with amusement and wonder, they closed the door behind them and stood beneath the lamps on either side.

"I told you, Lizzie, did I not? That man Mordecai knows his business, no doubt. I've spoken to Mother every time I've come!"

"You did. You did. I had my doubts. One hears so many stories, you know. Before tonight I'd half made up my mind that the entire movement was some sort of hoax, or the entire country had gone collectively off its rocker! But this . . ." And here the woman named Lizzie shivered, the light in her eyes changing to that of recollection. "What a strange thing. I'm so glad Peter is doing well."

"Perfectly fine," said her friend. "And now you may shun those horrid black dresses and find yourself another husband. The queen might seem to be planning an indefinite mourning period, but you are young yet and far too alone."

"I might stay that way!" said Lizzie with a laugh. "Go off on one of those big ships and see the world. Wear trousers and drink too much champagne. I rather fancy causing a scandal. That sounds like splendid fun."

Here, blessedly, they began to walk, still chattering, but Deadnettle, though he could hear them, was able to ignore them.

He crossed the street, strode past the front door and to the end of the long building. Around the corner, in an alley no wider than a carriage, a small door once meant for servants—still meant for servants, in a way—was set into the brick. "Where have you been?" Marigold whispered as soon as she was on the other side. She was ghostly against the slimy wall, the only light in the cramped, dark stairwell. "He came looking for you!"

"What did you say?" he asked, with a sinking feeling that he already knew.

"To use me instead. I'm younger, see, and stronger. Better."

All those things were undoubtedly true, but it was difficult not to feel slightly affronted nonetheless. Deadnettle shook it off. "You mustn't let them use you," he said. "If you can help it."

"Couldn't be helped this time, could it? Where were you?" she asked again.

He looked around, seeing none of the others. "Making arrangements to see our young friend," he said in the quietest of quiet whispers.

"When?"

"Tonight."

"Can I come?"

"You may."

She clapped her hands, and from down in the cellar came the rustlings of faeries stirring in the state of half sleep, half wakefulness in which they spent much of their time.

Resting, without using the energy required to dream. And they would not be dreams, but nightmares. Deadnettle made to move toward them. Marigold touched his arm. "Yarrow left us," she said. This was what they called it. *Left*. Because it was so much more pleasant to think of it as a choice, as a decision to leave this behind and go to a nicer place. Perhaps that's exactly what it was, too.

But whatever it was, it was happening more and more frequently. Deadnettle consulted the list in his head. Twenty-six, now, with the loss of Yarrow. From the hundreds in the old country, there are now twenty-six faeries left, every last one of them in this reeking, filthy basement. Of those, nine had been hatchlings at the time of the Summoning, the oldest, Teasel, now sixteen. He searched and saw her in a corner, combing out her long red hair with her fingers. He remembered taking her outside, hidden beneath his cloak, to practice her magic as it developed, and the pride when she had reached full strength.

Or as full as it would get in London.

Of the rest, ten had never seen their homeland, born here by the unique magic that created new faeries. And six were, while not quite as old as Deadnettle, wizened and sick, with barely the strength to open their eyes.

"Thank you," he said to Marigold, for there was nothing else he could. He would deal with Yarrow later in the same way he and Marigold had—eventually—dealt with Thistle. He would speak to Yarrow's beloved, Violet, later too.

"You'd best go upstairs."

Deadnettle gritted his large, sharp teeth.

It would come as a surprise to anyone learning of what was happening here that they were permitted to leave—but where would they go? The city was full of iron, and they had hurt themselves badly trying to cross the magical barrier Mordecai had erected.

Soon they had stopped trying. They stayed in their cellar, where there was no iron, and Deadnettle left only to deal with their dead, for Mordecai would not touch the faeries alive or otherwise.

Such excursions were exhausting. As was the sight that greeted him in the cavernous room. His kin lay huddled on streaked, torn mattresses, under scraps of blanket more hole than cloth.

In contrast, the faeries themselves seemed almost out of place, clean and shining amid the squalor. At first Mordecai hadn't cared whether the faeries ate or bathed, but it had taken only one wealthy madam to tilt her finely coiffed head and ask, in a delicate whisper, about the smell.

"Deadnettle?"

"Samphire." He patted her on the head, just above the ears that were showing the first hints of pointing at the top. It pained him to look at her in particular, the first hatchling to be born in the cellar, just a few short months after the Summoning. She'd be fully grown soon, would no longer look like one of the humans. Her indigo irises were expanding, drinking up the white around them as if it were milk. When she smiled, the faintest air of sharpness glinted at the tip of each tooth.

"Yarrow—"

"I know," he said. "I am sorry."

"And I haven't seen Thistle in days. Is he . . . outside?"

Deadnettle shook his head. "Him, too."

"But he was younger than I am!"

He would not explain to her, to any of them, the manner of Thistle's death. Far safer to let them believe it had happened in the usual way, for the usual reason. Even in telling Marigold the whole story, he had broken a promise made when Thistle—and Thomas—were yowling new hatchlings.

"I know," he said again. "I shall return soon."

There were no locks on the door at the top of the crumbling staircase, not physical ones. There did not need to be. At this hour, Mordecai would be in his private study, away from the lush parlors in which he and the other sorcerers *entertained.* Deadnettle passed through the kitchen and climbed the cramped, winding staircase—again, once used by servants when this had been a beautiful family home.

Some things did not change. In the grand scheme of things, Deadnettle had always been a servant, but back in the faery realm, he had been happy, privileged as one.

Oh, Wintercress.

He shook his head as he approached Mordecai's door. He would not allow himself to think of her here, for the sorcerer to take any more of the dead faery queen than he already had.

Mordecai Thrup was an evil man in a fine suit, made all the finer by the fathomless fortune his successful Spiritual Society had brought him.

"Ah, Deadnettle. You are late. I sent for you three hours hence."

"My apologies," answered Deadnettle, bowing low enough to hide his sneer. When he straightened again, his face was impassively blank. "I had business to attend to. We lost another in the night. Your performance was too much for him."

All of this was, broadly speaking, the truth, though the two facts were unconnected. But it was true enough that Deadnettle could speak the words without pain.

"Another? Was there not one just a few days ago? You must be more careful." The sorcerer smiled widely. "And I expect a new clutch of hatchlings a half year from now. We must replace the old with the new, if you insist on dying with such regularity."

Deadnettle took a deep breath. He had taken so many in this room he feared the evil was beginning to seep into him through his lungs, and it would be that, not the iron or the bells or the constant sapping of his faery strength, that would kill him. "I will see what can be arranged," he said through clenched teeth. "It is not, as you know, so easy for us. Hatchlings are born in quite a different way."

"This is not my concern," said Mordecai. "I ask for new faeries, you will provide them. Young, strong ones. The movement is gaining in power and numbers, and I am at its helm. All across London, people speak my name as the guide to the beyond, greater than Bellman or Lestrange or Wellington, and this new one, Jensen. The situation shall not change."

"One hopes," said Deadnettle, and it would take a sharp ear, a faery ear, to detect the insincerity in the words.

For a human, Mordecai had remarkably sharp ears. He looked up, dark eyes flashing beneath dark, greasy hair. He was clean-shaven, and this was unfortunate, for it allowed Deadnettle to see all of the malevolent smile now fixed upon him.

"I have been generous, Deadnettle. Your people are safe and fed. I keep iron and bells away, so that you may live in safety and comfort. The enchantment laid upon you is only one of many to which I could subject you."

You keep us here against our will, away from our home, snarled Deadnettle in his mind, his mouth clamped shut. *Tell me, what greater torture is there than that?*

"Trust me when I say, *faery,* that you do not wish to find out what else I could do to you. I ask little of you, of all of you. Do not make me demand more."

Deadnettle did not respond. What could he say? That there was nothing more the faeries could give; they had nothing left. To admit this aloud would be to give Mordecai an even greater power—the knowledge that the faeries had none and that the faeries knew it.

Deadnettle would not do that. Never. He would die first, in that rotten basement. Underground. A grave of the living.

"That little one . . . Marigold, did you say? I will never understand your ridiculous names. At any rate, she did well in your place today. I am pleased."

An ache grew in Deadnettle's chest. Marigold had seemed happy enough when she greeted him, but she was young and resilient. He knew she did not enjoy the process any more than the rest of them.

"I am holding another gathering in"—Mordecai checked an ornate golden pocket watch—"forty-five minutes. See that she returns to the blue parlor in thirty."

"You cannot use her again today."

"Oh, but I can." Mordecai was on his feet, rounding the large desk piled with ink bottles and heavy books. "I may do as I like, creature, and you would do well to remember that. You are here to serve me, not the reverse."

"She is tired," argued Deadnettle. Dangerous, yes, but while the sorcerer seemed not to care overmuch when one of their number . . . left . . . he would not put his own delicate hands to Deadnettle's throat. *Use me,* he nearly said, biting his tongue against it. He had an appointment to keep, one best conducted while Mordecai was occupied in the blue parlor and unconcerned with what the rest of the faeries were getting up to far below.

"Then she shall have a nice rest in the cage, shan't she? I grow weary of your obstinacy. You may go."

It was no great hardship to flee the sorcerer's presence. Closing the door behind him, aware the building, save for the study and the basement, were now entirely empty, Deadnettle went down the main, wide staircase. A cheeky luxury, a small revenge. Here, the floors were thick with carpet, the walls lined with fancy papers. Everything smelled of the silver and gold it had taken to buy each object.

Deadnettle wanted to scream.

On the ground floor, the doors to the many parlors stood open, waiting to be filled with humans and ghosts. Other such rooms were all over London, but these were different.

In these ones, it would truly happen.

He stood in the entrance to one, gazing at the sapphire draperies on the windows and around the polished oak table with its matching chairs. The people who came to sit at those chairs and visit with the spirits of their departed loved ones would feel the soft, plush velvet of the drapes brushing their knees on the way to the floor. They might rub it between thumb and forefinger to feel its richness, or remark on the beautiful color.

But they wouldn't know what was hidden behind. Mordecai would never let them see. That would reveal his secret.

And whichever faery he had chosen for the hour would lie, utterly still and silent, in the cage beneath the table. Smaller than the ones under the table on the stage in the grand concert hall, but big enough for a single faery, and for these intimate gatherings, a single faery was all Mordecai needed.

Oh, Deadnettle couldn't look anymore. He knew too well the darkness inside, the stillness and fusty air, the sound of the lock as the cage clicked shut.

"When are we leaving?" Marigold asked, dragging him to the farthest corner of the basement as soon as she spotted him, speaking in barely a whisper.

"I am going shortly," Deadnettle replied. "You . . . Mordecai has asked for you again." He did not repeat the bit about the sorcerer being pleased; it was no achievement to be proud of. "Yes, I know you are tired, dear one. But please do this for me. If he is happy, and busy, he will not think to speak to me again this evening. I can leave and return undetected."

Marigold pouted. "I want to meet the"—her voice dropped lower—"changeling. Properly, I mean."

"You will. Soon. This, I promise you."

"Go, then." She held up one finger and ran off, came back a moment later with his cloak. "Be safe. Stay away from the churches. It is Evensong tonight. There will be more bells than usual."

Clever girl. How did she learn these things? Where did she find the energy? But curiosity is its own strength, Deadnettle knew. He was counting on it when it came to Thomas. And Marigold was yet young enough to be curious.

Once outside, feet dragging over stone, Deadnettle's darker thoughts consumed him. Now was the time to fear that the boy would not come, or that some danger had befallen him during the hours since Deadnettle had sent him the note. It had perhaps been a mistake to give the child so much silver, but the coins were the only birthright that could be returned to him. At least the boy could set eyes on his mother's face, even if just etched in profile and unknown to him.

It was, equally, the time to fear that the boy *would* come and that Deadnettle would have to tell a story he suddenly wished he could avoid. Thomas had been raised by humans; he was only marginally more trustworthy than they were.

Deadnettle would be early, but that was preferable to the alternative. The lamps lining the path to the middle of the enormous park were blinding spots in the night and stung his sensitive eyes, but they'd be helpful to the boy. This was the only place in all of London where Deadnettle's breath came easy, the pain lessened by as much distance from any iron as possible. The lush green lawns almost, almost reminded him of home, in their vivid naturalness. He had once nearly decided to bring the other faeries here, escape with them and live in peace, but it was not a peace that would have lasted long. Mordecai knew about iron, and bells, and that they couldn't pass his magical barrier to flee London itself. It would not have taken him long to find them.

And Mordecai knew this place well.

There, fifty yards ahead, were two trees grown together, with a gap between just wide enough for a faery to slip through. The gap in which Thistle's sad, last breath had been drawn. Deadnettle would not ask the boy to try tonight, but he would show him. He would explain.

He would beg, if he must.

CHAPTER EIGHT

The Meeting and the Truth

THE COINS WEIGHED THOMAS DOWN. They were not so very heavy as all that, but never before had he watched every man and woman, lord and lady who passed him, one hand gripping tight to the satchel. To be fair, he'd never before seen anyone he thought might *be* a lord or a lady, but surely some of these fine people who passed him were, so fine were their clothes and carriages.

London spread around him, somehow much larger now that he was in the very center of it, the bustle of crowds around him like a swarm of so many bees.

Finding a place to lay his head had been a challenge. Snowflake note in hand, he had walked the city, yawning after his sleepless night, unsure where he would be safe. Out of doors was much too dangerous, no matter how firmly he held his bag. And if he were to find a soft, feather-filled bed in one of them fancy hotels, he might sleep right through to the next day, or the next week, and not meet the person who had sent him the note.

That he must do. That person held the truth, cupped in hands that might be strong or dainty, smooth or calloused. Might be human . . . or not.

Old ones, old ones, old ones.

He was sure, in the scouring light of day and with some time to think, that he didn't believe the fortune-teller or anything Lucy had said. But it was a pleasantly fanciful notion, and regardless of why, someone was leading Thomas on an adventure the likes of which he'd never had in his short, dull, dingy life.

Whoever was leading him on this adventure had also filled Thomas's belly with so much food he felt rather ill at the moment. At every stall or barrow he passed, he traded a perfectly ordinary copper penny or shilling for whatever they were selling. Unfortunately, this made him want to sleep even more, for hours or days or perhaps even a year, and not wake up until someone kissed him or pricked him with a pin, like in one of the stories Lucy had sometimes told him before bedtime, when he was too young to go out to the graveyards with Silas. But that had been years before, five at least, and Thomas was too old for stories now.

The graveyards . . . that had been it. The graveyards were how he knew London, and how he had thought of where he could safely close his eyes for a short time.

The nearest large one had been a fair ways away. Thomas trudged on, past shops and theaters and houses with rosebushes still slumbering from winter beside their stoops.

At long last, he reached the gates.

He had always felt comfortable in graveyards. Watched, yes, never alone, but the presence was always soothing. The crimes Silas committed, and made Thomas himself commit, were not the fault of the bodies buried within, for they were just trying to sleep too.

He'd made a good choice. The folks buried there must've had coffers full of gold while they breathed, and spent it on the big slabs of marble that formed small buildings. Tombs. Thomas found one tucked away whose flowers were bedraggled, neglected, bitten again and again by frost. No one had visited here in an age, and likely they wouldn't today. He fished in his pockets for his tools and clicked open the lock, rusted from weather.

The smell inside was too old to be bad, just stale earth and the merest hint of something sweetly rotten. When he closed the door behind him, the darkness was absolute, as was the silence.

As was the feeling he was not alone.

"'M not here to rob you," Thomas whispered, feeling a fool, but unable to stop himself from speaking. "Just need a sleep. I'll leave soon."

All right, Thomas imagined a cracked, dry voice answering in his head. The air settled and warmed, or Thomas told himself it did. From his satchel, he took the bundle of clothing to form a nice cushion. Cobwebs brushed his arms, and the space between the coffin and the wall was scarcely wide enough for him, but it wasn't much harder than the blankets he'd slept on before, and it was better'n anywhere else he could've found even if he'd searched London the whole day.

He awoke when the sun was setting, though he didn't know this until he pulled open the door and peered outside. The red light and the fug of soot that hung over everything made the city in the distance look as if it were on fire. He was alone, as far as he could see, any visitors to other graves having headed home for their suppers.

It wasn't time yet to go to the park—what an odd place to meet—nor did Thomas have anyplace else he needed to be. This was as comfortable as anywhere, as much *home* as anywhere. More than, if he'd truly been found in a grave himself. Had someone put him there because they knew it was safe and he'd be found soon? Or had someone put him there knowing the ghosts would watch over him?

Or both?

He counted the hours by the ringing of the church bells. "See, didn't steal nothing," Thomas said, standing, his satchel once again over his shoulder, clothes wrapped around the silver coins. "Sleep well."

Thank you, answered the imagined voice.

Neat paths had been laid between the graves. Thomas wandered up and down, reading names and dates. This, more than Lucy's tattered books, had been what'd taught him his letters, to string them together into words. Into people. He always read their names right before plunging the shovel into the earth, if he could.

Whatever they said, he was keeping the shiny coins. His, now, weren't they? He'd found 'em, even if someone'd left them there to find. Thomas dared not hope the answers would be more than that, that the person would know about who he was and where he'd come from.

He bought himself a pie going cheap from the back of a wagon and ate it on the way, the thin soles of his boots feeling the cobbles from Gracechurch Street to Mayfair. Perhaps he should buy a new set of shoes with his riches. The wide expanse of green lay before him, and as he neared, the Serpentine River shimmered in the moonlight. Thomas kept to the path, stopping only to stand beneath a flickering lamp and read, once more, the now-grubby bit of paper.

There, just there were two trees grown together, and was that a man beside them?

"Hullo," said Thomas.

"Do not be afraid," said the figure.

It turned and pulled back its hood.

Thomas couldn't stop his gasp. It looked . . . well, p'raps like a man, if you weren't inspecting too closely. But the ears were pointed and eyes much too bright, as if with fever. No white showed at their edges; no dark floated in the middle. Below, the teeth that showed through the smile were long and sharp.

"Do not be afraid," it said. "I swear an oath. I am not here to harm you. My name is Deadnettle."

"Nobody's name is Deadnettle," said Thomas before he could stop himself.

This only made it smile wider. "Mine is. I think you will find, Thomas, that my name is the smallest of strange things I am about to tell you. We might have a problem if that alone is too odd for you to grasp."

Its words were strong, with a hint of humor, even, but there was something a bit wrong about them too. It—the creature—was nervous and trying to hide it. Well, Thomas couldn't blame it for that. Nobody liked a coward, Silas always said. And he would know.

"Isn't," said Thomas defiantly, feeling anything but defiant. The fortune-teller screeched inside his head, chasing out the imagined voice from the graveyard. "Right, so that's your name. Who are you? What are you? And how do you know who *I* am?"

It was not quite the proper question. *Do you know who I am?* was what Thomas truly wanted to know, and he was suddenly, chillingly, certain it did.

The thing named Deadnettle edged closer. Now that it moved, it seemed old, frail. Its steps were weak and halting. Its hands shook ever so slightly before it noticed and clenched them into fists.

"Well, that is one thing sorted. You know I'm not human. That's a good start."

"Old one," whispered Thomas.

"Indeed. Faery, if you wish."

"You're real."

"I am. Real enough to tell you a story that you will not believe, or want to. It is, however, true."

"The fortune-teller—"

"Was right," Deadnettle finished for him. A good thing, as the park and the city and the entire world around

Thomas seemed to be spinning altogether too quickly. "Now, in fairness, she was right because she said the things I told her to say. She was rewarded for her part in this. Have no fear of that."

"But I'm not—I'm not a faery," Thomas said. He was just a boy. Not special in any way at all.

"That's not quite true," said Deadnettle. "You are not *magic*. There is a difference, and while I do not often hope that I am wrong, this is one of those rare occasions."

The ground wobbled under Thomas's feet. "Wrong about what?"

"Come. Sit."

There was a bench nearby, thick oak planks and beautiful iron scrollwork. The faery winced as they neared it. Thomas could just about think of him as a *he*, now, and not an *it*, and he gestured for Thomas to sit, but did not do so himself. Instead, he knelt on the grass in front, knees creaking beneath his robe, and folded his hands carefully in his lap.

Thomas watched him, his pointed ears and pointed teeth. The skin of his face was much too thin, showing strangely curved cheekbones and a ridge right down his forehead, stopping between his near-glowing eyes.

"Your mother was queen of the faeries," said Deadnettle suddenly. "Her name was Wintercress, and she was my dearest friend."

A tiny part of Thomas wondered for an instant whether this might be enough. He had wanted to know where he came from, and those few words said everything while explaining nothing. So easily, he could slip past this Deadnettle creature and run. Live off the coins until the last copper was spent and then return to Silas and Lucy, or not.

Of course, it was not enough. Nowhere near. He'd come this far, and if the best he got out of it was a story full of cobblers, well, that'd be better than nothing.

Especially when the story made him the son of a queen, a prince. He liked the sound of that. He'd always liked that sort of story when Lucy'd told them at bedtime.

Thomas didn't move. Neither did Deadnettle, who appeared to be waiting for Thomas to make his decision. Only when Thomas shifted his satchel farther onto his lap did the faery begin, once more, to speak.

"Wintercress was both kind and brutal, fair and as shifting as the tides. Powerful, oh, yes. Her ancestors— your ancestors—had ruled the faery realm since the dawn of time, and done it well."

"Where is she now?" asked Thomas, who had noted the use of *was*.

"She is dead," said Deadnettle simply, and the light in his eyes flashed brighter for an eyeblink. Then it was gone. "She was one of the first to die, after we . . . came here."

"And my father?"

Thomas wasn't sure that twist of the lips could properly be called a smile. "You do not have one. Our kind are different. It is down to the mother, who gathers the magic of the elements together in a, well, a ball of magic. Something like an egg. It is why our young are called hatchlings. It takes an immense amount of power and energy in an ordinary case, but it took even more where you are concerned."

"Oh," said Thomas, who didn't know where human children came from. Far as he knew, it wasn't much different. "Why did she die, if she was so powerful?"

"*Because* she was so powerful."

Deadnettle had been right. Thomas didn't believe a whirling word of it, but it was a shocking fine start to a story, and he found he wanted to know the rest. "How d'you mean?"

The faery took a deep, lung-rattling breath. "There is a . . . man, who lives right here in London. A sorcerer, a magician, a devil, call him what you may. His true name is Mordecai, and somehow, Mordecai taught himself how to summon us from our home, bring us here. Greed, it was, simple greed. You see, we have a gift humans lack, and wish for. It is not difficult to imagine that one might decide to use us for it, if one could only learn how."

"What gift?"

"The ability to speak with the dead. Or, to be precise, to let them speak through us."

"Ghosts, you mean?"

"If you like. So, Mordecai brought us here and trapped us. He cast an enchantment that closed the many doors back to our home for good, so we may never return. He keeps us in this city . . . this city full of the iron of industry and the bells of your churches, both of which are poison to us. Every day, we grow weaker. Every day, we lose more hope that we will ever see our beautiful faery realm again."

"So what happened to my—" Thomas could not say *mother*, not yet. That'd make it look like he believed it. "What happened to Wintercress?"

Deadnettle stared off into the distance, the fires of London burning around the edges of the park, chimney smoke twisting up toward the stars. Thomas waited.

"She had a plan, a plan to save us. It was her duty as queen, she said, and certainly there was no one else who could even attempt it. It had not been done in many hundreds of years, for it was dangerous and there had been no need. We lived such a peaceful existence for so long, far from the ways of humans or anything that might seek to harm us. We could move between the worlds as we wished, but as the trains and machines and metals came, we came through the doorways less and less, knowing it made us ill to do so. But none of this answered your question, did it? She cast a spell, a risk at any time, but she was already weak, and she had just had a child. It was enormous magic, an incredible danger, and she knew precisely what it would do to her. Nevertheless, she did it anyway."

"A child," said Thomas. "But there are two of us. I found his body. I had a brother, too."

"Not . . . exactly," said Deadnettle. "There *became* two of you. But the boy I left in that grave for you to find was not your brother, Thomas. His name was Thistle. You know this. I watched you read the note, and that small act alone gave me more hope than I thought I would ever muster again. Thistle is the reason you are, as I said, not magic. You are what we call a changeling, and at any other time"—he loosed his hands and spread them wide, careful, Thomas noticed, not to bring them near the bench—"you would be useless. A curiosity to be gawked at and discarded. A necessary tool in creating a very powerful faery, but a tool that has no function after the deed has been done."

Thomas wished he had thought to spend some of the faery's silver on a cool lemonade, his mouth went that dry. "The fortune-teller said I was broken."

"Very neatly split in two," agreed Deadnettle calmly. "There is a reason you are a faery but you have no magic. Thistle had it all, concentrated inside of him, and you are simply what's left. Ordinary, unremarkable. We each have those parts inside us, whether we wish to confess to them or not. Please," he said, placing long, inhuman fingers on Thomas's knee, "do not misunderstand. As I said, I fervently hope I am wrong about this. I would very much like to discover that the power of your royal line is within you, the last of Wintercress's blood. You see, Thistle died trying to reopen a gateway to our home, one that only a faery of the royal line may open. Do you see that tree, just there, which was once two trees that have grown together? Do you see the gap between? You are our only remaining chance."

Great iron bells began to toll across the city, ringing out over the park. Deadnettle's eyes widened in pain, and Thomas didn't care a jot. Whether faery or human or something in between, something curious and useless, the blood in his veins turned at once to stinging ice and hot, bubbling anger.

"Toss me away like rubbish until you decide as you need me? Was that her decision, or yours? It killed him, chances are it'd kill me, too, wouldn't it?" he asked, jumping to his feet and starting to walk as the faery clutched his head. Several yards away, Thomas stopped to look over his shoulder. "Thanks much for the silver."

CHAPTER NINE

A Dream

*W*ake up, Thomas, and hear me. Wake up, please!
Help us. You must help us. I know you can hear
me if you will let me inside your head. You are the
only one who can. I have left you everything you need.

CHAPTER TEN

A Change of Heart

THOMAS SLEPT THAT NIGHT IN the softest bed he'd ever felt, or touched, or even seen. Like sleeping on the fluffiest of summer's day clouds, wrapped in covers baked with as much warmth as the sun. He'd never rested so well, deep and dreamless.

They'd looked at him a bit funny downstairs, but there was nothing the slightest bit odd about the pound he passed the man in his silly uniform, who did not keep his job by asking too many questions, even of a young boy in tattered clothing who sauntered in and asked for the poshest room in the place.

He saw no reason not to spend that old faery's coin on whatever he liked. Figured he and the other one,

Wintercress, owed him a good night's sleep in exchange for his first night upon this earth, spent cold and lonely atop a grave.

Serve them both right if he decided to live like the prince he apparently was, on their silver.

He got it, and breakfast, too, when he awoke to bright daylight. Eggs and buns and kippers, all on a tray with a pot of tea and a dainty silver sugar pot. If Silas were here . . . But Thomas left it where it was, and its dainty spoon, too.

His dreams had been very odd, which he supposed was only to be expected. Again and again, he had reached for the doorknob of his room, only to find it locked because he wasn't opening it the proper way. And every time he opened it wrong, a great, terrible pain coursed through him.

How dare that Deadnettle think he'd a right to ask Thomas for help, after what the faeries had done? He knew he hadn't gotten the whole story, neither, but perhaps if he'd not run off, Deadnettle would've told him the rest of it. Then again, maybe he wouldn't. Those bells had seemed to pain him enormously, so much that he'd not said a word or tried to chase as Thomas ran off.

Angry as he was, it was sad nonetheless, if it were true. That being here caused the faeries such pain, and they would never be allowed to leave. The bells *had* seemed to cause him real agony. Sad, but Thomas shrugged in the fancy mirror, framed and everything, that hung on the papered wall. Nothing he could do about it, even if he liked to. He wasn't magic in the least, and trying to send them home had killed Thomas's . . . had killed Thistle—yes, that was its name—who was supposed to be such a powerful faery.

Thomas dressed in clothes that felt much grubbier than they had the day before, after he'd slept a night in such a clean bed. Downstairs, he skirted ladies in powder and petticoated gowns and a small dog that yapped at his heels for one of the strawberry tarts on a tray by the door. He gave one to the mongrel—the blasted thing near took his finger off in its haste—and kept one for himself, nibbling the scalloped edges as he stepped out into the sunshine.

It was . . . strange. If a soul'd asked him a scant week before what Thomas would do if given as much time to spend at leisure and as much coin as he needed to make that leisure enjoyable, Thomas would've had a list.

He stood on the corner, away from the carriages pulled up outside the hotel, and pondered.

He didn't believe it, any of it. And if he did, that didn't mean he had to help. Every last one of the faeries could go eat an onion. But . . . he wanted to see.

Mordecai, Deadnettle had called the man who kept

them captive. It wasn't so common a name as all that, and there must be even fewer of 'em who ran places where people could go have a nice chat with a ghost.

Turning back into the hotel, Thomas walked up to the desk. The dog came to nip at his ankles more, growling and snarling now. Beasts had never liked him much, but bully for them. He didn't like 'em either, so there. "'Scuse me," he said to a different man from the one who'd given him a key the night before. "I'm looking for a man named Mordecai. Famous, I heard, for . . . what's it, that spiritualism business. Somewhere over in Shoreditch. D'you know where?"

The chap behind the desk eyed Thomas curiously before his eyes flitted to a spot just over Thomas's shoulder. A bejeweled hand in a silk glove touched Thomas's arm. "Did you say Mordecai, young man? Darling fellow, just darling. Helped me speak to my daughter and my dear mother. Nellie, do stop barking. He's over Shoreditch way, as you say." She told him the streets, that he'd know the place soon as he saw it. "Have you lost someone, you poor dear? Speaking to them will help, I assure you."

Thomas blinked. "M-my mother," he said. It was true enough. "My brother, too." Which was not, really.

"Oh, you poor, poor thing. Tell Mordecai the Lady Huntington sent you. He'll see you, sure enough."

"Thank you," said Thomas, touching his forehead so she knew if he'd been wearing a cap, he would've doffed it. Lucy would be very pleased with his manners, if she had seen. All those lessons had not gone to waste.

Shoreditch wasn't terribly far, and for the moment the rain held off, though in London that didn't mean a thing. He could be drowned as a fish in an hour.

Just wanted to see, he told himself, setting his steps in the right direction. Not that he expected to see Deadnettle again, or wanted to.

Except that he had so many questions.

None of which were worth asking, of course. He'd just get more tales strange and tall as crooked houses and another reminder that he'd not been needed once the spell'd been cast. So they'd put 'im in a grave for Silas and Lucy to find, and sometime after, visited with a bag full of the same silver that nestled within Thomas's satchel.

It was all simply too much to believe. Too much to want to believe, just as Deadnettle had warned him. But the bit about them tossing him away and Silas and Lucy taking him in, that must be true. They had been the ones to tell Thomas that, not Deadnettle the bizarre, frail faery.

This city was filled to busting with more people than ants in an anthill, and Thomas'd never felt quite so alone. Not one of the folks who trotted and skipped around him as he walked, and certainly not one of the strange creatures Deadnettle claimed.

It took some searching when he reached Shoreditch, but it was not so large an area, and the streets were not as crowded here as they had been around the hotel. Between a boarding house and a large home now rotting with abandon, he found it. Once, twice, he read the small, elegant plaque beside the door, which gave very little away, and yet was clearly intended to advertise feats of wonder.

But Deadnettle had not called its proprietor a spiritualist; he'd called the man a sorcerer and a devil. Thomas raised his hand to knock and left it hanging there, right in midair, where anyone passing might look and think him simple.

There was a chance, a small but real chance, that everything Deadnettle had told him was the honest truth. And if it was, the gent behind that door was no gent in the least. No one Thomas wanted to look in the eye and ask about faeries.

He stepped back. Down the end was a corner, a likely looking alley where he might think for a moment. It was quiet, shielded from the sun at this hour. It'd seemed only clever to come here, but now he was at as much of a loss over what to do as he'd been after he'd been told his coins wouldn't pay to get him past Croydon by the man with the wobbly elbows.

To think Thomas had nearly left London. Small wonder Deadnettle had gently guided Thomas, sowing clues, dropping notes from the sky.

For Thomas was sure that was exactly what Deadnettle had done. How else would the slip of paper have landed so perfectly in Thomas's hand?

The red bricks were rough through the thin muslin on Thomas's back. Marching inside and demanding to see the faeries felt a dangerous, stupid idea. Returning to the soft bed, or to Silas and Lucy, sounded no better. He might never see Deadnettle again, or any of the others, whose names and faces Thomas did not know. They might leave him alone and resign themselves to the prison against which he leaned, thinking.

The quietest footsteps neared and turned the corner. Several books tumbled to the ground, thumping heavily but for one, which splashed as it landed in a puddle more mud than water.

The girl was young and very pretty. Thomas had never seen a girl with her hair down before; the ones he knew kept it in ribbons or plaits high off their faces. This one looked slightly wild, shock painted thickly upon her eyes and mouth.

Thomas thought he must look quite shocked too. "Look like you've seen a ghost," Thomas said, because it was the thing *to* say when faced with such terrified surprise. "Mary, ain't it?"

"I—I thought you were—" The girl swallowed. "Just for a moment, but you're not. Hello, Thomas. My name isn't Mary. It's Marigold."

So she was one of them.

"Why do you look . . . ? You're different," said Thomas when she'd led him to a hidden corner of a nearby square. *More like me,* he thought. *Not like Deadnettle.*

"When we are first born, we are called hatchlings," said Marigold. "After five years, we become fledglings. By fifteen, we begin to change. No one knows why, but when we are young, we look as you do. Wintercress used to say it's because faeries and humans were once the same, or so Deadnettle says. I don't know that I believe it, but I suppose it hardly matters. He said you ran away."

"'E told you?" asked Thomas, surprised, though he wasn't certain why. All the faeries might know about him. Only if that were the case, why the mystery and mucking about, and why had they met alone in the dark of night? It reeked of secrets and of truths that were worse, more terrible, than lies.

"Thistle was my friend," she answered, plucking at a broken buckle on her shoe. "I was there when he tried to open the doorway home again. I helped Deadnettle bury him and watched you find him."

He *had* heard something in the graveyard that night. Not just the whispering wind or the ghosts, always watching.

"And then you shared an ice with me," he said.

Her smile was very pretty, and very sad. "We needed to make sure you got to the fortune-teller, but I wanted to meet you anyway! Even if I couldn't tell you who I was. Thistle was my *best* friend."

"Oh," said Thomas. "I'm sorry."

"He knew what might happen. He wouldn't say so to Deadnettle, but he knew. He was a very clever, strong faery. He was ever making me laugh and gasp with the things he could do, silly tricks and terrific ones. He liked knowing he was going to be the one to save us, not because it made him more special or anything, he was too kind for that, but he saw it as his duty as a prince—as Wintercress's son. It was important, he said, that he do the right thing for his people."

"I don't understand why it didn't work, if he was so wonderful." It was stupid and selfish, but he suddenly hated Thistle—all the special, magic parts of Thomas himself.

Marigold narrowed her eyes. "The enchantment that

keeps us here is more powerful than anything we've ever seen before. Especially me. I was born here; I never saw anything back home. Just heard the stories. My mother used to tell me, before she left us."

Thomas guessed what she meant, and a rush of sympathy overtook him. He knew what it was like, not knowing where he came from, and it'd been confusing enough just these past few days. Marigold looked to be close to his own age and had never known anything else.

"Is it so very terrible here for you?"

She nodded. "It makes us ill and tired. Eventually too tired to wake again. The iron and the bells . . . ," she said, and shuddered. "We can sneak out, if we must, but few of us do. Really only me and Deadnettle, sometimes a few of the other fledglings because they can walk around among humans, like I can. I try to bear it by visiting the places I like and reading your human books. But we always come back. It's horrid here, but safe. The cage is the most awful part."

The cage. Thomas was afraid to ask, but ask he did, then wished he hadn't. At her words, he could picture it, the cage under a vast table, the faeries used to summon the spirits while the sorcerer pretended it was his magic all along.

He had seen the effect in the theater, if not the cause.

Like Charley said, just because a thing was strange, that didn't mean it wasn't real.

Just because a thing was awful, horrible, that didn't mean it wasn't real, neither.

"He doesn't have that kind of magic," said Marigold, "but we do. We are gateways ourselves; that's what faeries have always been. Because we can slip between realms so easily—usually—we may walk the line between the living and the dead, neither one nor the other. Some awful human will sit at the table and ask to speak to her kindliest aunt, and I have to find her and let her speak with my mouth, think with my mind so Mordecai can grow richer and richer. It's the most horrible thing."

Thomas's breakfast churned uncomfortably in his stomach. Sickening, indeed. But it wasn't the only thing that was. "She—Wintercress—she didn't want me," he said, refusing to look at Marigold as he did.

"That's why you won't help. Deadnettle told me."

"Would you?" he asked.

"No."

So surprising was her answer that Thomas looked her full in her clever, now smiling face. "You wouldn't?"

"Let someone use me after I'd been cast out as useless? 'Course not. That just sounds silly. Besides, I don't think you can. Deadnettle is desperate not to die here; it makes him foolish. If Thistle couldn't do it, I don't think anybody can."

Thomas got to his feet. "Show me the rest of them," he said. "I want to see."

Marigold made a great show of gathering her scraped, muddy books and pulling a threadbare scarf from around her neck. "You'll have to cover your face, in case any are awake."

Because they thought he was already dead. Of course. Even Marigold had been shocked, and she'd known of him. She'd *met* him. He held out his hand for the scarf. It smelled of moonlight and thunderstorms and ancient words.

"Wait," said Thomas. "Mordecai thinks I'm dead, too, don't he? That's why Deadnettle wrote I shouldn't speak to no one, and I should wear a cap, in the note he left?"

Unexpectedly, she smiled. "Deadnettle'll like that you worked that out. He was very pleased that you did as he said and didn't speak to anyone."

"Only 'cause I fainted," Thomas admitted. "I'd been planning it."

"You're quite like Thistle," she said, gazing at him before leading him back to the street on which they'd met and down the alley to a door.

"Why does he let you leave at all?" he said.

"Because he knows we have nowhere to go and what will happen if we let other humans see us. He believes he is kind." She helped him wrap the scarf about his head, leaving only the thinnest slit for his eyes. Even so, she put her hand in his. Her skin felt delicate as moth wings.

Down a staircase they crept, slimed brick on either side of their shoulders. Marigold released him to open another door, one into a large, open room.

Large, but not big enough to give the faeries within room to properly breathe, or live. Thomas gazed from corner to corner and along the walls, over the filthy floor covered with mattresses just as dirty. To think he'd once looked at the rooms he'd shared with Silas and Lucy as unfit. Lucy'd get down on hands and knees and scrub this place within an inch of its life before resting her head here.

But it seemed the faeries hadn't much choice. They themselves were clean and quiet. Most were asleep, or resting at the least. A few were gathered around stubs of tallow candle, the flame licking their faces. One opened its mouth, and Marigold put a finger to hers, shaking her head. It said nothing.

"That's Milkweed," she whispered, pointing. "Violet. Teasel. Whitebeam . . ." She named them all, and somehow it was terrible, knowing their names.

Thomas had seen enough. This and Marigold's tales of

what happened above were too much to bear. He ran back down the room and up the staircase, gulping in the shards of light that fell through the keyhole. He let himself out, back into the world of real, pleasant things.

If only he could forget what existed below.

She climbed up after him and stood close as he leaned against the rough brick wall. "All right," he said finally. "I'll help. Dunno how, mind you, so don't ask me. But I'll help."

Strangely, the first hint of faery he'd seen from her came with her wide, brilliant smile. No human could look quite like that when they smiled, all aglow, like a fire had burst to life within them.

"I knew you would," she said. "You *are* like Thistle. Thank you."

Thomas felt his face go red. *My pleasure* didn't seem the thing, somehow.

"Meet us where you met Deadnettle," she said, saving him from having to answer at all. "Tonight, when the bells chime ten."

It'd just gone five.

He left her there, a sad thing itself, but by the time he was out of sight, he was running. It took some time to cross the river and some more after that to find the familiar, grubby face.

"Charley!" Thomas called.

"Back so soon, old friend?" Charley hopped off the crate on which he'd been perched. "Lucy 'n' Silas will be glad to see you, though truth be told Silas was mighty glad of those coins, too."

Thomas shook his head. "You must come with me, Charley. You won't believe it. Not sure I do." Charley could be trusted with anything that wasn't a quid, and Charley'd pinch him if he was dreaming, if Thomas pointed at the faeries when they weren't really there. But why would Thomas dream of faeries speaking to him? "Just come. You'll see."

CHAPTER ELEVEN

The Second Test

T HIS TIME TWO CLOAKED FIGURES stood at the meeting place. They both turned at the sound of footsteps, much sooner than Thomas thought they'd hear them. The taller of the two, which must be Deadnettle, seemed about to run, but the other grabbed his arm.

Thomas's belly turned over when he and Charley neared enough to see Deadnettle's stony face, rage setting the green eyes to flame.

"Wotcher," said Charley. "Are you Thomas's family, then? Your eyes aren't half-strange."

"What is this?" Deadnettle hissed. "You foolish boy!"

"I am *not*," said Thomas. "You've got each other, you

and Marigold and the rest of you. Marigold was there when Thistle was trying, weren't she? I want my friend here. 'Sides, if you're going to show me all about being a faery, I'm going to show you that humans aren't all awful. You'll see."

Charley's eyes darted back and forth. "Human?" he whispered to Thomas. "Faery? What's this about, Tom?"

"It's a bit of a tale," Thomas began.

"I'll tell him!" said Marigold. Deadnettle was casting his gaze between the three, but his anger appeared to be melting away a bit. More than anything, Thomas thought he looked like he could use a good sleep. A week's worth.

"Fine," said Deadnettle grimly. "Thomas, we must test you."

"Better you than me, chum." Charley clapped his hand on Thomas's shoulder as Marigold tugged him away to sit on the grass. "I never was one for that schooling lark."

"Lucy used to set me tests, for my numbers and letters and whatnot."

"These will be . . . different," said Deadnettle. "Did you sleep last night, or were you digging up a grave? This will be easier if you are rested."

Thomas remembered the soft feather bed with no small degree of guilt, now that he'd seen where the faeries slept. "Yes," he mumbled.

"Good. We do not know what you are capable of, if anything. For a long time I believed that what Wintercress did with yourself and Thistle was known only in theory to be possible. Certainly no one had attempted it in living memory, and we live for a very long time."

"How long?"

"A few hundred years, on average."

"Will I live a long time? Longer'n a human?"

"I cannot say," Deadnettle answered. "Perhaps. Let us start."

"Um," said Thomas. "All right. What do I do?"

"The very basest, easiest of our magic. The wind is coming from the east; try to change it. I am not particular about direction."

"I beg your pardon?" Thomas asked.

"We may change the weather, if we wish. Your human stories of us discuss this sometimes, though one should never believe the stories—"

Thomas glanced to where Charley and Marigold sat. She was talking; he looked as if he'd been smacked with a fish. A great big trout from a barrel down at the market.

"*I* heard you do dark magic and steal human children."

Deadnettle's eyes burned with fury. "Dark magic? Do we seem evil to you? And as for the other . . . I can assure you I took no human infant when I left you in that graveyard. You are, indeed, a changeling, but humans have always been wrong about what that is."

"Always been wrong?" Thomas asked. "Does that mean I'm not the first?"

"There was a rumor of another, long ago. Very long ago. Because of you, I now believe it to be true. Now we return to the weather. It is not from the flapping of our wings—which clearly we do not have—but the elements of nature can be manipulated, very simply because we are elements of nature ourselves. In the faery realm, where we have the full might of our magic, it could snow on a summer's day or be the first crisp days of autumn for a year, if it struck one of our fancies. Concentrate and attempt it."

"Show me."

Deadnettle flinched and took a breath.

"Here," said Marigold, hopping easily to her feet to approach them. The winds changed, blowing into Thomas's face. "See? It's possible. Just try."

"Cor," said Charley.

"Give me another go," said Thomas.

"At your leisure."

Thomas tried, and tried, and tried again. It didn't seem to matter how often the old faery told him to concentrate, to picture what he wanted to happen. He grew warm with the effort and shame, for with each failure came a deeper frown from Deadnettle. The bells in the distance chimed eleven, then a new day. Overhead, the moon shone thinner than it had the night before, or the one before that. Several times, Thomas saw Deadnettle raise his eyes to it and lower them again, sadder than before.

It was no use. Thomas couldn't so much as twitch a leaf in the other direction. He wanted to. He *wanted* to help the faeries go home, but if a breeze was too much, how would he do anything else?

"Enough," said Deadnettle. "We will try again tomorrow. Marigold? We must go."

"I want to stay with Thomas. Just for a bit, please, Deadnettle?"

"We have been gone for hours. I cannot . . . The iron, Marigold. Come."

"You go, then. Mordecai will be sleeping, and I'll come back before sunrise. I promise."

They exchanged a very long look, which Marigold won. This Thomas knew. Lucy could silence even Silas when she chose to. Deadnettle nodded.

The three watched him leave, cloak sweeping over the grass. Thomas, and Charley, too, he guessed, quickly lost sight of him, but Marigold watched until he was surely out of the park and on the grimy London streets.

"So, is that all you folk can do? Change the weather?"

Charley asked. "I don't mind saying, I'd be happy with a year of Julys."

"It's the simplest. We start with that, and then the other skills come. I've always been a bit rubbish at weather, really, but I'm good at other things."

"What else can you do?" Thomas was curious, and it was easier to ask Marigold than Deadnettle. Indeed, there were many things he'd have liked to know, but asking her about Thistle might make her sad, and she was smiling.

"Watch."

And watch they did, as she silenced the birds in the trees with a blink and plucked a mushroom from the earth to turn it into a rose. Her ears twitched and she laughed— the queen, in her palace a mile away, was tickling one of her children. Marigold gathered a pebble from the ground and, in her palm, it turned to silver.

"If I could do that, I'd've been living on strawberry tarts my whole life," said Thomas, agape.

"Not if you didn't know you could do it, and you'd have to spend it quick. It changes back soon enough. It's simple." She blew on the pebble and a fine, glittering dust sprinkled the ground.

"Blimey. What can't you do?" Charley asked. His customary grin was in place, but Marigold's smile slid away.

"Touch iron, stand near to church bells, tell lies, harm

another living creature. Well, we *can* do those things, but they cause us terrible pain and make us weak and sick. Deadnettle says he's seen faeries die of it."

"You can't fib? Truly?"

Marigold nodded.

"Right." Charley clapped his hands. "I'm proper funny, aren't I?"

Thomas laughed. Marigold did too. "Yes," she said.

"And handsome. The handsomest to be found in London town."

"No."

"Oi!"

The laughter carried them along the path that led out of the park. Marigold slipped her hand into Thomas's, just as she'd done at the market when they'd shared a raspberry ice. Thomas and Charley kept up with their questions until Thomas felt he knew everything about being a fairy, 'cept, you know, how to actually *be* one and do what they did. He was most intrigued—and repulsed—by how they came to speak with the dead, or rather, let the dead speak through them. Their kind had always been able to do it, she said, but they were not born with the gift. It arrived slowly, in dreams at first most times, when some particularly loud or irritable spirit was looking for a way into the world. Soon, they learned to control it, so the spirits came only when called.

"D'you like to do it?" Thomas asked. "I mean to say, when you're not in a cage under a table?"

"I think people should be allowed to sleep," she said. Thomas remembered the theater and agreed with her. "*I like to sleep.*"

"So you need sleep, then," said Charley.

"Oh, yes. We think that's where the story of us stealing into people's homes to sleep in their beds comes from, but we would never do that. Deadnettle always says people make up stories that are the opposite of the truth because it's the easiest thing. Anyway, he couldn't do that. He snores. And Thistle was a proper chatterbox. Said more asleep than awake. Pity it never made sense."

Somehow, that made the old faery seem more, well, human. Not quite so scary. And it made Thistle feel more real. A missing part of Thomas. Marigold released Thomas's hand. "I must go back now," she said. "It was a pleasure to meet you, Charley. Thomas, we will try again tomorrow."

Smoke rose over London. There was no fire, but how Deadnettle wished there was. Gleefully he would set a torch to its rooftops and draperies and wooden doors and let it burn to ash, were it not for that he and the other faeries would be trapped inside. The boy seemed rested. Good.

He thought of Thomas asking whether he would live longer than a human. It was optimistic to believe the boy would live out the next week, and a week was just about what they had. Deadnettle examined Thomas's face for the familiar lines he had inherited from Wintercress. Odd that he had never done so with Thistle, but he had watched Thistle grow quickly from a squalling hatchling to an energetic fledgling and, finally, to a young but undeniably powerful faery.

And yet Thistle had failed.

"Marigold," Deadnettle said quietly. She heard him easily, fifty yards away, her hands full of the pebbles he had asked her to collect, and walked over. Once, she would have run, or skipped. He should stop bringing her on these outings, keep her away from the iron and preserve her strength, which was clearly being sapped from her. He certainly should not have let her stay out without him. Thomas, however, seemed more at ease in her presence, and Deadnettle could scarcely blame him for that. Iron was poison, but the silver of mirrors was not; he was aware of how he looked, or must to a human.

Not that Thomas was human. But nor was he a faery, precisely. He knew nothing of their ways, their customs. Every moment Deadnettle was near him, he could see the boy's eyes brimming with questions. Some he dared ask, some he did not, and Deadnettle was not going to prompt him. He would not lie—would not weaken himself further for such a useless purpose—but he would wait until questioned. At least Thomas had not brought the human boy along this time, and Thomas would soon be too occupied with other things.

"What first?" Marigold asked.

"The wind."

"Show me again?"

Deadnettle flinched and took a breath. He could do this yet, if he must. The leaves quivered in the still night for a scant few seconds. Deadnettle's shoulders slumped.

It would have been nice to pity the boy. A blush rose in the young cheeks, and his eyes squinted in concentration. For Deadnettle, a great many years ago, this had been easy, easy as taking a breath of the air in the faery realm. Pure, clean air, not the stinking soup of London. He had simply thought about it, desired it, and the wind had done his bidding. Now, as he watched Thomas clench both teeth and fists, it was almost possible to regret having asked this of him in the first place.

Almost.

And Deadnettle knew that before this business was done, he would regret far more than this trifling challenge.

"It seems . . . not," said Deadnettle, stopping him, unable

to hide the disappointment in his voice, though he would have kept it there even if he could. It might merely be a case of practice, of trying harder. Thomas *must* try as hard as he possibly could.

The night breeze blowing through the park was scented with embers and lily of the valley and iron. Iron that smelled of blood and sting. Church bells marked the quarter hours, making Deadnettle and Marigold cover their ears each time. Her ears were more sensitive than usual too, Deadnettle noted. He truly must make her rest more. A deep, long sleep, or as much of one as could be achieved in the cellar at the Society.

"My head aches."

"Something else," Marigold suggested, pushing herself from the tree against which she had been resting. "I showed him some of the other things, Deadnettle. Let him try one of those." Searching the ground, she soon came up with a pebble, and Deadnettle knew what she was suggesting. So, clearly, did Thomas, but she demonstrated the gift, the stone taking on a dull sheen.

"Well done, Marigold. Your turn, Thomas. You must think of what you want to happen. Wish for it with your entire being and purpose." *Whatever manner of being you are.*

He tried. With each attempt, Deadnettle felt frustration and hopelessness rise within him, wave upon wave. What *had* he been thinking, fetching the boy, going to such effort to lure him? Why not simply leave him where he was, in his filthy hovel, thieving from the dead? This was never going to work. The wind stubbornly refused to shift, and the pebbles stayed plain gray, and he could not turn a mushroom into a rose or silence a bird in a nearby tree. For that last, hope had lit one brief second as if the feeling were sunlight, but then the thing had begun twittering again, smug and taunting.

The boy had no faery magic. None at all, and this was the more damning to believe because it meant that Wintercress, darling, beloved Wintercress, had done exactly what she'd set out to do. She had not made a single mistake, left the faintest scrap of magic in the changeling when she had performed the spell.

So right, in that. So perfect. And yet, about Thistle, so wrong. Oh, he had been strong, yes. That was true. Had shifted the winds while still a newborn hatchling, younger than anyone Deadnettle had ever known. By the time he had neared the age of twelve, when all faeries reached their fullest powers, he was very nearly terrifying. All the more so because he'd been a gentle, happy boy when the weight of his duty wasn't burdening him.

He had covered the sun with the moon. Now the moon was fading, fading with each passing night. Deadnettle felt as the moon must, shrinking away bit by bit. He would never see the final day of April again. He would never be closer to his home than he was this very moment unless Thomas somehow succeeded.

Thistle had not been strong enough. That Thomas would be was a ludicrous wish, a desperate one, and Deadnettle clung to that desperation as he would a cloak to keep him warm.

There was no light in the cellar save a single candle, and Deadnettle could sense Marigold watching him by its light. Outside, dawn had long since broken, and sound from upstairs indicated that soon Mordecai would summon one of them for his first gathering of the day. By now the society ladies would have taken their tea and had their hair properly coiffed to venture out for a meeting with this dead aunt or that one.

Marigold maintained her gaze. Deadnettle shrugged. Well, let her. As with Thomas, he was not about to pester her, nor explain himself before he was asked to. It was mildly more forgivable in Thomas's case; he had an excuse for ceaseless questions, whether or not he voiced them. Marigold, however, should know better.

Deadnettle rose and checked, one by one, on the others. All the ones left. Mordecai had dragged more than two hundred faeries from their home, and despite his orders, new hatchlings had not been born at the rate older faeries had . . . left them.

It simply wasn't that easy.

At eight o'clock, when Mordecai was safely ensconced in his study with brandy and a pipe to celebrate another successful day, Deadnettle lifted the latch on the door, a silent Marigold at his heels.

"You're late," said Thomas. He seemed in good spirits. Excellent. Perhaps that would help. Indeed, perhaps that was a reason for Deadnettle's own lessening powers.

Church bells rang out through the night.

And those were another.

"Apologies," said Deadnettle, forcing a smile, finding that it came easier than some other forms of magic. "We cannot *quite* come and go as we please. Close, I grant you, but we must be careful."

"Did you have a pleasant day?" Marigold asked. It had certainly *been* a pleasant day, from what Deadnettle had gathered from overheard conversations as Mordecai greeted his guests in the Society's entrance hall. Warm, with a shining sun. But with each new degree of warmth, the approaching summer . . .

He shook himself. Good spirits. It was worth attempting.

"Well," Thomas answered, "I've been wondering, see. If my mum—this Wintercress woman—knew about this stuff and made Thistle 'n' me, why hasn't it worked? More, why can't we ask her? Do one of 'em séance things and get her to tell us what to do next. Been trying that business with the wind all day and I still can't do it."

It took quite some care for Deadnettle to keep his smile in place. *This Wintercress woman.* She had been a queen! But Thomas had never known her as such, never known her at all. He knew her only as a name and a face on a silver coin. "Because we can't," he said. "We cannot speak to those of our kind who have left us."

"Why not?"

"It is difficult to explain, particularly since we did not make the rules; we can only live by them. Did humans invent the sun or the turning of the seasons? No. But"— and Deadnettle found that, once again, his smile was very nearly real—"I choose to think that we live so long, when we finally die we don't wish to be awoken again."

"So, only humans, then."

Marigold giggled. Deadnettle stifled a groan, and Thomas stared at them both. "What's so funny?"

"Deadnettle had to bark like a dog for a whole half hour once." Marigold laughed again.

Yes, yes, it had been very amusing. Before she could get too carried away with the story, Deadnettle drew Thomas over to a soft-looking patch of grass and seated them. He explained, as best he could, that the faeries could only act as bridges between the lands of the living and the dead, but a bridge does not know the hopes and dreams and thoughts of those whose footsteps pass across it. A human soul would only venture over the bridge when called by another human and, yes, a dog by another dog. The horrible yips and yaps between the living one and Deadnettle had echoed through the whole Society. The snapping thing had kept trying to get under the table.

"Beasts don't like me, neither," said Thomas. Deadnettle blinked.

That was curious.

"So you see, Mordecai needs us, but, loath as I am to admit it, his presence is also necessary for what he forces us to do. Or at least, that of a human to do the summoning. Humans gather together in cities"—filthy, stinking cities rife with iron—"and dogs roam the streets in howling packs. All creatures wish to be with their own. And now we must get to work."

The air seemed to Deadnettle a touch less heavy, the stars brighter, and the moon also. And, oh, how he longed to say that it made a difference, the budding leaves on the trees bending to Thomas's will, a crop of mushrooms transforming to an entire bouquet of roses red as blood.

He longed to say that.

Once more, they parted when the moon was high overhead, another sliver shaved from its side as neatly as if someone had sliced it with a razor, its handle inlaid with opal or mother-of-pearl. Deadnettle often saw such things, shining in the windows of gentlemen's shops, and felt for the precious stones in their own metal prisons.

They were halfway back to Shoreditch when Marigold finally spoke. "You believe it will kill him. Trying to open the gateways. As it did Thistle."

There was no question in her voice, but there was anger, simmering, ready to bubble over.

"I think it's a possibility. A likelihood. You know the gateways can only be opened by someone of royal, magical faery blood."

"Yes."

"Thomas's is too diluted. This was the effect of the spell Wintercress cast. Picture, if you will, a glass of seawater. It is water, and it is salt. Imagine, if you will, pouring half the water into another, empty glass, but keeping all the salt in the first. Indeed, you do not have to imagine such a thing. You could do it, if you wished."

"The salt is the magic?"

"It is, and I am attempting to discover whether a few small grains remain within Thomas, without spilling a drop of his blood. I fear, however, that when we actually *need* his blood, we will have to pour out every last drop of . . . of water to find them. Even then, there may be none."

"Deadnettle!" She turned on him quickly enough to stumble on the slick cobbles underfoot, and he caught her by a thin arm. Glaring, she wrested it from his grasp. "Why start this, then, if we're going to fail?"

"For you—you and the others," he said calmly. Pain struck through him, sudden as lightning, and his knees shook with weakness. "And for me." Ah. That was better. Deadnettle breathed deeply. "I am the last of us born in the old country who both remembers it and is strong enough—just—to lead you, Marigold. Without me to guide you back, it is likely you will never find the way. And I . . . I should like to die knowing I did everything I could. I will live another two moons, three at the most. If, beyond hope and reason, we are able to return to our home in that time, it will heal me. Even a lessening of pain, I would be grateful for. But more than that, I *must* know we tried everything. Do you understand?"

Slowly, she nodded. "It doesn't seem fair."

"It isn't," he agreed. "If it comforts you, I believe he knows what is being asked of him. I will make certain of it, before the attempt is made. But we have not hidden what happened to Thistle, and despite being raised by humans, he is no fool."

Their footsteps slowed as they walked the long, wide street that would lead them almost to the Society. In heavy silence, they turned the corner into a narrow road and Deadnettle yanked Marigold into the shadows.

He'd heard . . .

Something . . .

"Deadnettle?" Marigold whispered, and he clasped a hand over her mouth, his ears pricking.

That was not Mordecai skirting the redbrick building; Deadnettle knew the sorcerer's footsteps too well. Nor was it another faery, who would be lighter, near soundless.

Marigold's eyes widened as she heard a locked window rattle in its frame.

"What are you doing in there, Mordecai?" asked the man to himself, to the night, which gave no reply. "What is your secret?"

Deadnettle knew that voice. He had heard it before, in a theater hung with mustard-colored drapes.

It was a voice whose owner could not be allowed to discover them. He would not free them. He would use them, or kill them as revenge on Mordecai. It was the voice of a human, and humans could not be trusted.

It was the voice of the spiritualist Jensen.

CHAPTER TWELVE

Dreams, Again

*N*o! *None of this is necessary, these foolish tests Deadnettle is having you perform. You do not need any of this, Thomas. You are different, and it is that difference that will save us. Wake up and hear me! You must go home, Thomas. The truth is there.*

CHAPTER THIRTEEN

Blood and Bark

THOMAS AWOKE IN COMPLETE DARKNESS. He pushed the door of the tomb open a crack and a blade of daylight fell across the floor.

He'd made it rather plush in here, if he did say so himself, with a blanket thicker'n all the ones he'd slept on his whole life put together, and two thick pillows besides. Food, he could find anywhere, apples and pies from barrow-men and market stalls. His fingers searched the little pile in the corner and came up with a lump of cheese, which made a nicer breakfast than Lucy's watery gruel any day of the week.

Whoever rested—eternally—in the tomb didn't seem to mind Thomas being there. It felt, well, *friendly* was the word for it. He'd enough coins in his pocket to spend every night of the rest of his life in that posh hotel, but it felt wrong, what with the faeries in their cellar, and so he'd returned to where he'd slept before meeting Deadnettle that first time.

Besides, some nosy parker at the hotel might've wondered where Thomas was getting his shillings, called the coppers on him, and Thomas was very good at slipping in and out of graveyards unnoticed.

He peered out through the crack. A branch, studded with new leaves, cut across the sliver of sky. Thomas gritted his teeth and concentrated, keeping his eyes open, hard as it was, so he'd know if he'd done it.

No such luck.

But it wasn't luck, was it? It was skill, a faery skill, and Thomas wasn't a faery. Not a faery and not a human. Something strangely in between, entirely alone.

"I'll come back later," he said to the coffin, as he did each time he left. It felt the polite and proper thing to do. *As you like*, he imagined it whispering back to him. If he was a proper faery, maybe it really would.

Steering well clear of Shoreditch—however amusing it was to think of what the mad sorcerer would do if he saw Thomas walking about in daylight, looking for all the world like a dead faery—Thomas walked through

London, a London quite unlike the one he'd always known. It was an odd thought, that there could be lots of different cities layered one over another to make one whole one, like a cake in a bakery window. There was Thomas's London, of nighttime and graveyards and filth, and this pretty one, with spiky roofs and houses white as sugar and ladies in taffeta.

There was the faeries' London too, a prison whose iron spires were as burning needles to their skin and whose bells rang out like rifle shots.

The river ran under his feet. Thomas leaned against the railing in the middle of the bridge, peering down. Thistle was down there, Marigold'd told him. That's what they did with the ones who *left*. Graves got dug up, as Thomas well knew, and hidden things got found, but no one was going to rake about on the bottom of the great black Thames.

"Hullo, Charley," said Thomas, nearing that selfsame pond where Charley liked to sail his little boat. But there was no boat today. Charley was sat on a rock at the edge, halfway through an enormous mutton pie.

"Thomas!" Gravy sprayed onto his shoes. "Hullo, mate. How're the faeries? That Marigold's a corker. Funny thing, ain't it, them being your family, and that whole business about the other one. 'S'like you're dead, but not. Not many people as get to walk around eating sausages during the afterlife. Least, I don't think so."

"That's the truth," said Thomas, for they were his family. Marigold and Deadnettle, and Wintercress even though she was dead, and Thistle, in an odd sort of way, and all the others he had only glimpsed, but whose names he knew. And whom he wanted to save.

"You should come home, y'know. You could still help the faeries, but Silas and Lucy'd be right pleased. I told 'em you could look after yourself and you'd come back soon, just like you asked, but they's worried."

Lucy, Thomas could believe. "Silas tired of doing all the digging 'imself?"

Charley laughed. "Not going to say that ain't a part of it, now that you ask. I helped him out last night, two pairs of hands being better than one, you know. Gave me something to do, seeing as I can't sail my boats in the dark, but he kept going on about 'finding my bones.' Says I'm not near as good at it as you."

Much as he'd disliked the grave robbing, Thomas allowed himself a smug smile. He had been good at it. Many an evening there was food on the table because he'd picked a good one after Silas'd turned up nothing but dirt and worms.

"Listen," Thomas began slowly, unsure of quite how much to tell Charley of the story. "If you had to do something proper dangerous, but it was the right thing to do, would you?"

163

"Gracious, Thomas, what're they asking you to do? S'pose that'd depend on what it was, y'know. Ain't been a tight spot yet I couldn't wriggle out of, and there've been plenty! But coppers haven't nicked me so far." He lifted his pie as if raising a mug of beer, then took a large bite. "Long may it continue."

Thomas shook his head. It wasn't that sort of danger. Deadnettle hadn't said as much, but Thomas was no fool, even if he couldn't do their poxy faery magic. Trying to open the doorway had killed Thistle, hadn't it?

"You all right, Thomas?"

"Tell Silas you've got some other business tonight. Come back to see the faeries with me. This magic business isn't working, and you just said yourself, ain't never been a spot of bother you couldn't escape. It's like hands, ain't it? Two brains is better than one."

It felt to Thomas as if there were two halves of him walking back across the bridge, shrunken by the hugeness of the river and the buildings ahead. Like the city itself, split in two by a thick line. He could go tell the faeries to eat an onion; they'd chucked him out, so why help them when it could be the end of him? But if he *could* do it, he'd save the faeries *and* show 'em he was better than the special one, the one they'd kept. He just needed a bit more practice, is all, to get the hang of the magic business. There'd never been a thing so far he couldn't learn. Lucy'd said he'd taken to his numbers and letters faster than anyone she'd known.

And that Mordecai chap, he was human, not even half a faery, and he'd managed to learn some kind of magic, powerful enough to open the gateway and trap the faeries in London.

Well, if Thomas had time, p'raps not much of it, and more coin in his pocket than he needed, he was going to spend both. He whiled away the afternoon in a theater of amusements, candlelight catching on the gilt and paste as tumblers flipped about on the stage and a man made a wooden doll talk with his own voice.

Thomas paid very, very close attention to the magicians and illusionists, leaning forward in his seat, eyes on their hands. Right, so it was a different sort of magic than what the faeries had, but it *was* magic. Things did not always have to be what they seemed. Stories did not always have to be believed. Rules could always be broken.

After that, he had himself seated at a table laid with proper linens and silver, promising the waiter that his mum would be there to join him any moment. Curiously, however, she hadn't appeared by the time he'd cleared his plate of sizzling steak and fried potatoes, or scooped the last of the ice from a china bowl. The man went so far as to offer to help Thomas find her, but Thomas silenced him with a shiny half crown and dashed when his back was turned.

The moon and the sun were both in the sky, one rising, one falling. He counted the time by the church bells once more. Thomas made his way to the park, picking his way through the elegant city folk enjoying the spring. He was early, but they'd turn up soon enough. Alone, he practiced bits of faery magic, or tried to. Over and over, he tried all the things they'd showed him. This was why he hadn't asked Charley to come to the theater, just so's he could have this bit of time to himself.

"What *are* you doing, Tom?"

Thomas jumped. A stone dropped from his hand. "Er. Um."

"Well, that explains everything, that does." Charley grinned. "Or not. You're trying that trick with the silver, ain't you? Can you do it? Because if you can, I'll run off and spend it quick, as Marigold said."

Thomas shook his head. There must be a trick Deadnettle and Marigold weren't telling him, something they'd forgotten because it was, as Deadnettle had said, as ordinary to them as breathing.

But their breaths, when they arrived, were not coming easy. Darkness had covered the grass only a few moments before; they must've run the whole distance from Shoreditch.

"Oh, Thomas," said Marigold. Her pretty face and clever eyes were fever-bright.

"All right?" asked Thomas, though she clearly wasn't, and Deadnettle neither. He'd not yet seen the faery look so weakened. "I've been thinking. I just need some more time. I know I can learn to do this."

"That is just it," said Deadnettle through dry, cracked lips, ignoring Charley. One of his pointed teeth had made a cut; a spot of dark blood crusted the corner of his mouth. "There is no time."

"Where's the big hurry all of a sudden?" Thomas asked, taking in, again, their tiredness and labored breathing. Why had they run here? "You've told me 'bout this nearing of the worlds business, but I can't see as another night or two makes a difference. What's the rush?"

"I fear we will no longer be safe even at the Society," said Deadnettle. "If one may call that *safe*. Another spiritualist is endeavoring to discover Mordecai's secrets, a man named Jensen."

"I've met him," said Thomas. "Just the other day, at that theater you sent me to. He helped Lucy when I took ill."

"Did he? Yes, I wondered if that had been you he spoke of. Regardless, if he does learn what Mordecai is doing, there is no telling what manner of hands we might fall into. It is difficult to imagine one crueler than Mordecai himself, but I have had many long nights to do so. No human has ever given me reason to trust one, and I shall not begin now."

"You left *me* with humans."

"On Wintercress's orders, not by my own choice. Please, Thomas. I ask this of you. Try. Any one of us can do the things we've been trying to teach you. It is unimportant, small magic. But you are of the royal line, and only you may open the gateways now. We must try tonight."

"Tell me what to do," he said to Deadnettle. A large tear dripped down Marigold's cheek.

Thomas had always been very good at doing what he was told. Be rather nice, he thought, if he hadn't had quite so much practice at *that*. It'd be a funny thing if Silas and Lucy'd prepared him more for this than Deadnettle and Marigold had managed thus far.

But Deadnettle spoke first to Marigold. "Be ready," he said. "If it works, be ready to fetch the others and take them to the nearest. You know where it is."

"Yes, but—"

"Enough."

"Steady on," said Thomas. The full weight of what he

was about to attempt descended upon him, heavy as if it were made of iron. "I want to know something first." This might well be his last chance to find out. "Tell me about the night I was born."

Deadnettle twitched with impatience. "There is no longer time."

"I say there is," Thomas said, standing tall.

"He's right, Deadnettle."

The scowl turned the faery's face ugly. "Oh, if I must. Wintercress told me she was going outside, to see the moon. You were born on the last night of April, a year after the Summoning. A year to the day, and she wanted to see the moon that night, she said, because it meant we were closest to the faery realm once more. There is a night, at the end of October, when the human world is closest to the land of the dead. In April, it is closest to the land of the faeries. I knew she was weary; we all were, for that was the night of Mordecai's grand performance, his first grand performance, and we had only just returned to the cellar. I followed her and watched as a hatchling was born. She said words in our faery tongue, words no one had used in living memory, and one hatchling became two."

"Blimey," said Charley. Thomas agreed this summed it up.

The strange tree loomed over them. Through the gap, Thomas saw a distant lamp sputter out.

"I must have said something, exclaimed my surprise. She beckoned me over, and I could see how weak she was. She could not lift you, either of you. She told me what to do, where to take you, and to keep Thistle. She said he would be ready to open the gateway when he covered the sun with the moon. And those were the last words she ever spoke to me."

"Thank you," said Thomas. "Tell me about Thistle, too."

The merest hint of a smile twitched Deadnettle's bloodied lips. "For that, I defer to Marigold."

"He was quite like you," she said, stepping forward. "Or perhaps, you are quite like him? I'm not sure. He was funny, and brave, and kind."

A tiny spark of warmth flared inside Thomas. Marigold thought *he* was those things as well.

"He didn't always like that he had been born just to save us. What, Deadnettle? It's true. He liked mushrooms and milk."

So did Thomas. He couldn't think of anything to say. It grated upon him even now, rough and stinging, that he had not been the kept one, but then, it hadn't worked out so well for Thistle, neither. The whole tale was sad.

"Are you ready, Thomas?"

More tears dripped down Marigold's cheeks. He nodded and stood.

It was just a tree. A mere tree. The bark scraped and scratched and caught at his shirt as he wedged himself into the space. Deadnettle's eyes were two points of starlight; Thomas could not see Marigold's. Perhaps they were closed. Charley stood in the shadows, awed into silence, which served only to show how strange everything about this truly was.

He thought of the story Deadnettle had just told him. He was the changeling, the useless one, but there was no argument that he was Wintercress's kin, of the royal line to whom these gateways belonged. Deadnettle neared and passed him a silver knife.

"I cannot harm you," said Deadnettle. "You must do this yourself."

One slice. Two. Blood slipped and poured from burning lines across his palms, through the calluses from nights of holding a shovel. Thomas placed his hands against the tree. He concentrated, filling his head with everything Deadnettle and Marigold had told him about the faery realm. He spoke the words, words that could be written only in strange, spiky letters and came off his tongue sounding strange and spiky too.

The world went dark.

Thomas Marsden was twelve years old the first time he tried to open the gateway to the land of the faeries.

He blinked and opened his eyes. The darkness around

him was only a bit lighter than the one now easing in his head, which didn't half ache.

"Where am I?"

Immediately, a face hovered over his own. He knew that face. Large eyes and pointed teeth. A name, a strange name . . .

"Deadnettle," Thomas said. The face smiled, near enough. A second face joined it, and everything returned to Thomas in a rush. "Did I do it? Did it work?"

The smile fled. "No. But you are alive. That is something. I do not know why, and that is something else."

"Wait," said Charley. "You were 'specting him to die?"

"I was."

"Gracious, and just when I was starting to like you. Tom—"

"So was I, Charley," said Thomas. "But I'm right as rain, see?" He tried to sit up and fell back to the earth again. "Mostly."

Long fingers gripped his wrists, turning his hands over for inspection. "I do not . . . Your blood, it is different. . . . Something . . . The spell . . ."

"I can try again," said Thomas, willing the stars overhead to stop moving quite so much.

"Deadnettle, I need to speak with you," said Marigold. "It's important."

The faces disappeared. Slowly, Thomas pushed himself up, his whole body sore as a bruise, hands on fire but no longer bleeding. His hearing was nothing like as good as the faeries', but it didn't need to be.

"Repeat yourself," said Deadnettle in a cold, flat voice.

"Thistle didn't do it. You said Wintercress told you he'd be ready when he covered the sun with the moon. But he didn't do it, Deadnettle. He couldn't. He tried and tried, but he couldn't do it! And then I read in an almanac that it was going to happen anyway, an eclipse, humans call it, so we told you it was Thistle."

"But you told me he had. You both did. You . . . *lied*, Marigold. This is why you've been so weak. I have blamed myself for this, needing your assistance these past days, bringing you out amongst the iron and the bells. And Thistle! Thistle, with all his meaningless chatter of honor and duty. Where is the honor in this? Where is the duty to which he felt so bound? Ground into the muck of this stinking city, that's where. Do you not see what you did? If Thistle hadn't been weakened when he tried, perhaps he would have succeeded! We might already be home!"

"I know," she said, miserable but curiously strong. "But you aren't the only one of us who is desperate to get out of here, and don't *you* see? Even without any magic, Thomas has already managed more than Thistle ever did. He lived.

He spoke the words, and bled, and he lived! He can open the gateway, Deadnettle. I'm sure of it."

"I am not." Deadnettle spat on the ground. "I am certain of nothing anymore, except that we shall all die in this forsaken place. And as far as I am concerned, it cannot arrive quickly enough. Come, Marigold. We will go back to the others and discuss the doorways; it's been some time since the last. Perhaps one of them has a new suggestion."

"But Thomas—"

"Can be of no help or use to us, I'm afraid. He may keep his remaining faery silver, and his silence. Tell anyone about us, Thomas, and I will see to it with my last breath that you regret doing so. For you, too." He pointed at Charley, looked up at the sky, at the moon. "Farther away," he muttered. "Always farther away."

The church bells rang, and Deadnettle stifled a scream. His last breath might not be so very far, it seemed. Each chime appeared to pain him more, each step he took to exhaust him deeply.

"I'm staying here," said Marigold. She tore two strips of cloth from the hem of her cloak. Bandages.

"As you like. I no longer care. Good-bye, Marigold."

Thomas sat, agape, as Deadnettle stormed away.

CHAPTER FOURTEEN

Punishment

D EADNETTLE SHOOK WITH FURY.

How *dare* she? She and Thistle both! They had ruined *everything*. If Thistle had only waited until he had managed the feat Wintercress had foretold, they would be home now. Home, which would ease his agony, if not heal him entirely.

But no, the foolish fledglings had lied to him, weakened themselves, and caused this tragedy.

He knew that was unfair. But as he had told Marigold, he no longer cared. The gateways were closed. Wintercress and Thistle were both dead. He himself was the only one left who had come from the faery realm. And now someone who was as near a human as made no difference knew of them. Thomas had been raised by criminals, in a den of thievery and thuggery. What would happen to them when he or his friend decided they must no longer keep his knowledge of the faeries secret? Knowledge that was even more extensive than Mordecai's, because of everything Deadnettle and Marigold had told him.

He stood, and pain rattled through his body as his legs gave way beneath him, every bone bruising against the hard basement floor. Some of the other faeries shifted restlessly on their beds, glowing eyes blinking open for a moment before they closed again.

Panting, Deadnettle crawled into a corner, curled there against the wall. He would have to wait for her to return, and in the meantime he would summon the energy to punish her for disobeying the very rules of their people.

How *dare* they.

By dawn, she had not yet returned. Worry mingled with Deadnettle's rage, a rage that felt as close to strength as he'd had in many months. Soon, a burst of fear joined them, striking deep within him at the sound of the door opening at the top of the stairs.

More quickly than he would have thought possible, Deadnettle jumped to his feet, and he was halfway up the steps when he saw the polished toes of Mordecai's leather shoes.

"Ah, Deadnettle. Good morning. Would you be so kind as to fetch that lovely Marigold for me? I have an early appointment."

Mordecai did not attempt to pass Deadnettle on the stairs, and this was a very good thing. He did not like to descend fully if he could help it. The conditions in which he kept the faeries were all that much easier to deny to himself if he did not cast eyes on them himself, Deadnettle was sure.

"She is sleeping."

"So wake her."

"I will not. You have used her far too often in recent times."

Mordecai cocked his head; Deadnettle mimicked the movement.

"One of the others, then."

"Use me," said Deadnettle. "I am yet strong, Mordecai, and right here."

"Oh, all right." Mordecai checked his gleaming pocket watch. "Come, then."

He shouldn't, but Deadnettle's anger at Marigold would never stop him from protecting her, protecting any of them. This he would do with his last breath, as Wintercress had done, and any faeries before them who had ever been called upon to do so. This was another one of their rules.

In the plush hall above, Mordecai stopped so abruptly Deadnettle came within an inch of running into him and reeled back in disgust. He braced himself against the wall so the sorcerer wouldn't see how he shook, and cleared his face to disguise his horror.

"If I didn't know better, Deadnettle," said Mordecai slowly, dangerously, "I would think you were keeping the young ones from me. Are you trying to keep them strong? Are you plotting to escape, perchance?"

Deadnettle took a shallow breath, in and out. "Of course not. Where do you think we would go?"

"I have wondered that. You must know the doorway to your land is well and truly closed. My greatest piece of magic, my greatest achievement. Perhaps you think elsewhere in Britain might be more hospitable to you, even if you were to break through my barrier, but I tell you, Deadnettle, there is no corner of this great land not touched by the revolution. Iron is everywhere, and where it is not, the bells of the devout keep your kind at bay. This is, and will always remain, your only home." His dark eyes burned through Deadnettle's thin skin. "Especially yours."

Deadnettle could say nothing to this, his greatest fear given voice. That he would die here, away from the faery land, and that Mordecai knew it would happen before too long.

Who would protect the hatchlings and fledglings then?

Or the ones who survived until they were old and weak?

He trembled anew, with sickness and anger. Not only at Marigold and Thistle now.

"We are in the green room," said Mordecai as he opened a door, his warning delivered. "Get inside."

Falling to his knees was easy; Deadnettle was far more concerned with how he might get up again once the session was over. He parted the curtains around the table and grimaced at the cage underneath. Big enough for a full-grown faery, long as it had no desire to stretch.

A thin blanket padded the bottom. Deadnettle curled atop it and tried to ignore the click of the lock, but his ears were one of the few faery strengths left to him. He heard the group of ladies—and one gentleman, unusual—talking about the adventure ahead when they were still two streets away, and the opening of the front door was as loud as if it were right beside him.

"Come in, come in," said Mordecai. Bathed in darkness, Deadnettle could hear the man's false smile, and hear it become real as the guests passed a fold of money. "Are you prepared to communicate with the beyond?"

"Oh, yes," they chimed together. Footsteps neared. The chairs around the table hissed against the rug as they were pulled out. Mordecai closed the curtains over the windows and lit a candle with a snapping match strike.

"Join hands, please, my honored friends," said Mordecai. The man could put on a performance, there was no denying. "We must show the spirits this is a warm, safe place for them to visit with us for a spell. Clear your minds of any sad thoughts, banish all that is unwelcome."

If only that were possible. Deadnettle grimaced. He was still too enraged. He must calm himself too.

Or . . . not.

"Good people of the afterlife, come to us." Mordecai's voice was a low drone now. "There are several here who wish to commune with you in kindness and light. First, the lovely Clarissa Baker, who seeks her dear, departed father. Father, are you there?"

Deadnettle could see him, the father, in the part of his mind that faeries kept for such things, the window into the realm of the dead. He was smiling, and Deadnettle was quite sure his daughter wished to know this.

Deadnettle clenched his pointed teeth, and his lips over them.

"Aha. Perhaps not just at the moment." The toe of a polished shoe slid beneath the curtains around the table and nudged the cage.

No. Deadnettle would not surrender. He had had *enough*. Watch what would happen to Mordecai's famed Spiritual Society if every last faery refused to speak.

"We shall try another. Mr. Baker, please visit with us when you are ready. For now, the lovely sister of this fine gentleman, Marcus Parrott, would you please come to us?"

Deadnettle could see her, too. Tearstained and alone in a mass of mingling spirits. She opened her mouth. Deadnettle bit his tongue.

Mordecai tried another and another. His shoe pressed against the cage but could do no more than that without alerting the guests to the presence of something beneath. Fury boiled off him like heat from a stew, and in the darkness, Deadnettle smiled.

"It seems the *spirits* are not talking today," said Mordecai, attempting to laugh. "This happens, on occasion. I assure you that if you return—"

"Knew you was a fraud," said the other man at the table. "Never believed in any of this tosh, but my wife insisted I try. She wants the brooch that badly. That was half a month's rent, Mr. Thrup, and I'd ask kindly for it back."

"Indeed," chimed in a female voice. "I shall go to one of the other Societies who have had success."

"No, no, I insist that you return another day!" said Mordecai. "It will be better then. You have my word!"

"The word of a fake? I think not," scoffed the same woman. "Our money, if you please."

Paper banknotes whispered against one another as

Mordecai counted them out and returned them to their rightful owners. Moments later, the front door slammed and the sorcerer returned.

A strange calm stole over Deadnettle. When the lock snapped open, he climbed out to face his fate.

He screamed and screamed. So did the others.

Through burning eyes, Deadnettle stared down at the iron chains binding him, twisted about his legs and arms, wrapped like a noose around his neck. There was no lock, but there hardly needed to be. He couldn't shake them off. The rest of the faeries huddled together in the farthest corner, fully awake for once, clothed in pain and horror. They could come no closer, and they would not make it if they tried to escape through the grating.

Deadnettle tried to regret what he had done, but the agony was too great to be generous, even toward himself. The fire raged through his head, blocking his ears and nose, and raced along every bone.

"Deadnettle!" Marigold pushed open the door from the servants' staircase and caught sight of him, closely followed by Thomas. She had brought him back here! Again! "What did you do? Oh, Deadnettle!"

She was beside him, pulling at the chains and stifling her own screams, fingers slipping at the knots as every faery part of her fought against touching the metal. The scent of her singeing flesh broke through Deadnettle's haze.

"Stop!" he ordered. "Stop it! Get away, all of you!"

"But—"

"Listen to me!"

This would kill him soon. The knowledge was almost a comfort.

"Move!" said a voice. A young voice, a boy's voice, but it sounded so like Wintercress in its clever fierceness that Deadnettle dragged his head up fully straight, the chains shifting against his neck.

Thomas pulled Marigold's scarf from his face and pushed Samphire out of the way. "Don't move," he commanded Deadnettle. Quick hands, neither faery nor human, tugged at the chains, loosening them and casting them into a clanking pile. It hurt, oh, it hurt, but Deadnettle braced himself and felt cool air touch his charred skin as each link left it.

Finally, finally, he was free. Samphire and Milkweed caught him before he could fall, laid him gently on a mattress. The iron grew more distant, rattling in Thomas's arms as he carried the chains through the door and up to the top of the staircase that led to the alley and dropped them there with a slithering *clank*.

"Shhh, Deadnettle," whispered Marigold, and from her

mouth came a stream of words in their old, spiky faery tongue, so rarely used here because it made them so homesick. Smoke stopped rising from his wounds. Their edges began to knit together.

And stopped.

"It's all right," he told her. This was as much as she could do; such magic wasn't simple at the best of times. "Leave it. I'm all right." He wasn't, but that didn't matter now.

"Deadnettle, *why?*"

He waited until Thomas returned. He had something to say to the boy, but he couldn't yet. "I had a . . . disagreement with Mordecai. It seems"—he looked at her—"that I must quarrel with everyone today."

"I—"

He reached out to touch her face, the effort near unbearable. "We will find another way. Do not worry. Thomas, thank you." The searing marks on his skin still felt like chains, as if he couldn't move.

"She had a thought," Thomas began, and got no further. The door at the top of the main stairs swung open. Polished shoes hit the first step.

"Hide!"

It was either admirable or utterly stupid that the boy stood his ground, Deadnettle's mental scales tipping slightly toward the former as Mordecai appeared.

"Deadnettle, you live." The sorcerer was clearly disappointed. "I thought perhaps when the screaming stopped . . . Who removed your chains? Which one of you did this?"

"I did." Marigold stepped forward and held up her injured hands. Deadnettle saw the pain flash in her bright eyes at the lie, but Mordecai did not. "Why did you do that to him?"

Anger seethed on Mordecai's face just for an instant before he controlled it. "A difference of opinion," he said soothingly to her. Deadnettle wished for the strength to stand and strike him, but it didn't come. "From now on, there will be no leaving this building unless you are with me. I have barred the windows and doors with the iron you so loathe. You may rot here with your dead. I hope this serves as a lesson to you—"

Deadnettle knew. The moment Mordecai fully saw what was right in front him was plain as day on his evil features.

"I knew it," screamed the sorcerer. "You have been hiding them from me, Deadnettle. The strong ones! Telling me they slept or were spent! You told me this one was dead! You lied! I thought you beasts couldn't do that? Hmmm?"

Silence rang through the basement. Deadnettle opened his mouth and closed it again. There was no safe thing to tell him, or way to explain. He'd end every one of the faeries himself before he told Mordecai of a spell that would split one faery into two, one of them more magical, more special than his brethren. Marigold trembled with panic, and Samphire placed her hands on Thomas's shoulders. They dropped away to her sides as he walked right up to Mordecai.

"I was," he said, completely calm.

Deadnettle blinked. *Oh, good boy. Oh, you very clever boy.*

CHAPTER FIFTEEN

A Means of Escape

I WAS," SAID THOMAS AGAIN when Mordecai didn't respond. "They brought me back. We can do that, you know, if the magic's just right. Marigold and I made a plan, ages ago, that we would, if something happened to the other. We can do it to anyone. Only if we're well rested, though. It takes quite a lot of energy."

"Anyone?" Mordecai breathed.

"Anyone," said Thomas firmly. The other faeries chimed agreement. Deadnettle nodded solemnly.

"I will be richer than I ever could have imagined. Think of it! Jensen and the others will never know what hit them now. I shall be famed the world over! Marvelous. Marvelous! I shall cancel the sessions for the week. Plans must be made! You must rest. Fresh food will be left for you shortly. Prepare yourselves. And"—he pointed to Deadnettle—"please do not forget what happens if you anger me."

With that, he fairly flew back up the stairs, slamming the door behind him. Footsteps thundered overhead.

"Goodness," said Samphire.

"That was—" Marigold began.

"Exceptionally clever," said Deadnettle, who dragged himself to standing and limped over to Thomas. "I may have been quite wrong about you. You have your own kind of magic."

Thomas's eyes went to the painful burns covering the faery. "Touching iron isn't magic."

"Perhaps not," Deadnettle agreed, "but I am beginning to see that *different* may not be such a terrible thing."

"I could've told you that from the start."

Some of the faeries laughed, a sound that had its own magic, too, for Thomas knew how rare it must have been these past many years. Deadnettle properly introduced the faeries Marigold had once pointed out to him, and now it didn't seem quite so awful to know their names. Samphire, Teasel, Woodrush, Milkweed, Violet. Each one smiled at him. Violet was very small, half as high as Thomas, but she fixed him with such an intelligent look he stepped backward.

"Hello, Thomas. Goodness, you really do look just like Thistle. I never really believed the bit about changelings, but here we are," said the one named Woodrush, or perhaps it was Milkweed.

"I can get you home," Thomas told them. "I know I can. If he"—Thomas pointed up to the ceiling—"can open the gateway, I must be able to. Goodness, he's horrible, ain't he?"

There was no arguing with this, but, "There is the slight difficulty that we are now trapped here, Thomas," said Deadnettle. "We are no longer allowed to leave, which Mordecai allowed for us to dispose of our dead because he does not like to touch us if he can help it. I imagine it makes us too real, if he were to do so, and he might be forced to think of what he does to us."

"You're trapped. I'm not," said Thomas, smiling. They could not touch the iron that now apparently barred the windows and doors, but he could. "Though 'e'll be keeping a closer eye, to be sure." Thomas inched through the gloom to one of the slimy brick walls. "You blew silver to dust. Can't you do the same to these?"

"To nothing made by human hands," said Marigold.

That made sense, inasmuch as anything about all of this did. "Right, then. I've another idea, but best if I wait here a bit."

He was given the cleanest mattress on which to sit, and the candle moved close by so's he could see in the dim. Marigold sat to his left, Deadnettle to his right. Fresh food had indeed been left for them at the top of the stairs. Thomas ate a few small bites to be polite, but left the rest for the others. "Tell me about the faery realm," he said, and listened.

It was . . . not like hearing a story he'd heard before, as such, or listening to someone recount a memory, but Thomas found that he could picture Deadnettle's words easily. More easily than expected, for a land on which he'd never set eyes. He could see the hills and the valleys, the shimmering lakes and not a scrap of iron anywhere. The faeries lived in huts of stone and grass and spent their days gathering food, amusing themselves and one another with their magic, playing beneath the sunlight and the stars.

And now they were kept locked in cellars and cages. Thomas felt ill.

That was the other thing. "There," said Deadnettle, "we do not sicken. If injured, we heal. This is why our bodies are strong enough to live for centuries; they are never weakened."

"Will it make you better, if you can get back?"

Deadnettle paused, then shook his head. "I do not know. I suspect the damage is already too great, but I would be thankful enough for the pain to leave me. The others will heal."

Thomas listened more, as if to Lucy telling him a story at bedtime, as Deadnettle spoke of how the faery realm came to be. The old faery's voice was weakening, and he grimaced each time he moved, but he did not stop. Once, the faery realm and the human realm had been one and the same place, layered one on top of the other, as Thomas had just the day previous thought of London. Humans had come, and they and the faeries had lived together in peace.

For a while.

But they had brought iron with them, forged it into blades and tools. Smoke from their fires and steam from their smiths choked the faeries, and their hills were flattened by shovels. And when it was discovered that the faeries could speak with the dead, they were seen as evil.

"So our queen—not Wintercress, then, but one before her, and from whom you are descended—performed an extraordinary feat of magic and sent our land away from this world. Her name was Hazel, and she left gateways, just in case they were ever needed. The trees that share her name, though not all of them. A few very special ones. And her magic was such that she made it possible only for those of the royal line to open and close them."

"And I am the last," said Thomas.

"You are."

"Then how did Mordecai do it?"

"I have long wondered. I can only guess that Hazel was more knowledgeable about faery magic than about human skill. Humans have long tried to move between the worlds. We are kept here for that very reason. Mordecai would have no Society if it weren't for that desire, and Mordecai somehow gained the knowledge he needed. That is all I know."

Thomas's eyes felt heavy, and his mind, too, full of thoughts. He curled on the mattress as sleep stole over him, thick and dark. Dreams shifted like the wind he could not move, full of voices. One voice. But though he strained and strained his ears, he could not hear its words.

He startled awake. The candle flame shone yet, much lower than before. By its light, he saw the other faeries, asleep, some with their eyes open. It must be late enough now that he could safely leave.

His foot was on the first step, his set of lock picks taken from his satchel and held tight in his hand. They'd served him well, opened countless graveyard gates. Marigold touched his shoulder. "What are you going to do?" she asked. Thomas squinted and saw Deadnettle watching them, listening too.

"I've spent my years so far as a grave robber," Thomas

said, a grin forming. "Reckon digging is the same any-where. Wait for me."

The windows of the little house glowed from the hearth fire within. Thomas raised his hand, ready to knock, but that was daft. It'd been his home for years, hadn't it? He turned the knob and heard a gasp louder than the crackle of the flames. An instant later, Lucy had squashed him to her, and for a moment, just a moment, everything that had happened since Thomas had left felt like a dream. A dream full of voices.

"My boy," she said, squeezing him even tighter before letting him go. Silas sat at the table, lacing up his big boots. Charley dropped his fork. In the corner, Thomas's pile of blankets waited just as he'd left it, ready for him to come back. It had been quite a long time since he'd last slept, and they had never looked so inviting. But there would be time to sleep later.

"I need help," said Thomas, looking right at Silas. He felt Lucy's eyes on him. "Please and thank you," he added.

"Aye, do ye now?" said Silas. "With what, may I ask?"

"Digging," Thomas answered, and again he smiled. When it came right down to it, digging was much more useful than turning a rose into a mushroom, though he'd take the silver pebbles bit if it came to him. "I'm sorry for running off, truly I am, only I had to find out. And I have, and they need help." The whole way here, Thomas'd wrestled with how much to tell them, but Silas was going to see the truth for himself soon enough, leastways if he agreed, and he'd tell Lucy. Charley knew already. Thomas told them the story, every bit of it, and did his best to ignore the gawping.

"This better not be a load of cobblers, boy," Silas said, fetching his shovel.

"Who could imagine such a thing?" whispered Lucy. "Those poor creatures. Whatever will you do with 'em once you've dug 'em out?"

Ah. That plan was, well, not scuppered as such, but not fully formed yet in Thomas's mind. "I'll think of something," he said. "Mordecai's going to go right around the twist when he figures I've lied to him. We don't have much time."

They'd never had much time, not since the whole business began. The worlds were drifting apart, and Deadnettle was dying, and Thomas didn't know what to do. But he remembered Deadnettle watching him with new eyes, calling him the king of the faeries. He was. He would save them, somehow.

Laden with shovels, Thomas led Silas, and Charley, too, across the river. As Charley had rightfully pointed out, three pairs of hands were better than two, and this was going to be backbreaking stuff. Not even digging into a grave in the dead of winter was as bad as this'd be.

But he'd done that a hundred times over. Surely that added up, neat as the sums Lucy used to set.

The sign for the Shoreditch Spiritual Society gleamed dully. Thomas scowled at the ring of iron around it, though it didn't hurt him. Silas whistled under his breath at the poshness of the place. "Cor," whispered Charley.

"Need to make sure this one's empty first," Thomas said, pointing at the house beside, separated from the Society by a narrow alley. "Deadnettle thinks so." And it looked it, crumbling and dark, the paint on the window sashes flaked to nothing.

Charley withdrew a set of slim metal picks from a pocket. "Simple as Simon." The door creaked open on hinges in sore need of oil. Dust billowed up from the rugs under their boots.

It was a grand place, however, despite the neglect. Cobwebs wove over marble, and beetles had chewed their way through finest oak. "Shameful, this is," Silas grumbled. "A palace like this rotting empty while some folks as has to do with much less. Shameful."

That might well be true, but it was convenient. Thomas hardly fancied digging from the next road over. "We must find the stairs to the cellar," he said. His voice echoed through the empty rooms.

Once they did, Thomas near wished they hadn't. The cellar reeked of rotten potatoes and mold, the stench making his eyes water. He'd have liked to pinch his nose, but no digging would get done if he did. He supposed he'd smelled much worse, deep in the graves, though he wasn't usually buried in them himself. The walls closed around. A match flared, and a lamp sputtered to life.

Walls. Thomas turned, pointed to the one they needed. Hoisting his shovel with its iron blade, he struck hard at the brick. Rescuing the faeries with iron. Now, there was a thing.

Silas and Charley took up their places beside him; the noise was suddenly immense. He hoped it wouldn't wake Mordecai, next door and somewhere high above the cellar. If it did, well, he had Silas and Charley with him, and they could do things faeries couldn't. Things with heavy iron-bladed shovels. "I'm sorry," Thomas said through the din, sure the faeries would hear him.

"Still not sure I believe any of it," Silas said between blows with his shovel. Bricks fell away around their feet. "All sounds like nonsense from a story, if you ask me."

Thomas bit his lip and tried hard not to shout as his shovel fell on his toe. It *did* sound like a tale, something from a book. He would think of that later. His muscles ached and the calluses on his palms, allowed to rest for a few days, burned again. "There's silver at the end of it, I promise you," he said to Silas and Charley. "That's what matters, ain't it?" He'd always thought that's what mattered to Silas.

Silas paused, panting, a sheen of sweat over his reddened brow. "You think I like our business, boy? Let me tell you, sometimes you do as you must for there to be stew and coal, and you try not to think of it too much." Silas struck again, and a wall of earth cascaded down.

Coughing, blackened, they cleared the rubble into the middle of the cellar. Dirt was easier going, huge scoops of it flying through the air. It muffled the smell, at least. Charley whistled a tune, jaunty and too bright for this dark place, until Thomas's shovel hit brick once more with a loud *thunk*.

"Move back, far's you can," he ordered through the wall. No sound came back, nothing to do but hope they'd heard, hope they'd been woken by the noise of the digging. The iron would likely still hurt them, but leastways he could make sure they didn't get too close.

Brick by brick, Thomas, Silas, and Charley chipped away at the mortar. Quieter now, with lighter strikes, so's not to reach Mordecai's ears or harm the faeries'. "Remember," Thomas told them, "you can never tell a soul about this, hear? Not even when it's said and done."

"Whatever you say, Thomas," said Charley, grinning. It was plain on his face that he, like Silas, didn't trust the story Thomas'd told them and was waiting to see what was truly on the other side of the wall. All manner of riches, perhaps, gold and silver and jewels. Thomas bided his time, working away at the tough, aged bricks. They would see.

The first one was pried away; it fell with a clatter and broke neatly in two. On the tips of his toes, Thomas stretched to see, but the space was too high. Silas loomed over him and his shovel fell away.

"Well, I'll be . . ."

Fast as they could, the three made a hole large enough for a man—or a faery—to slip through. In the Society's cellar, the faeries were crouched along the opposite wall, fearful and cringing from the iron, but Thomas smiled and looked at their work. He'd made one gateway. He'd make another. Casting his shovel aside onto the pile of earth, Thomas stepped inside. He turned to make sure Silas and Charley did the same before they followed.

It was not so easy for human eyes to adjust to the gloom here, but slowly enough, they did. Silas blinked.

"Oi," he said, pointing. "I know you."

Deadnettle rose, unfolding to his full, tall height. "Yes," he agreed. "You do."

CHAPTER SIXTEEN

An Unheard Voice

Y*ou were so close, Thomas! So close to what I left
for you. You are awake. Why won't you listen to me?
Just like something from a story, yes. Remember that.
Listen to me, and remember!*

CHAPTER SEVENTEEN

Tales and Truths

YOU BROUGHT HUMANS HERE?" Deadnettle
demanded of Thomas. "It wasn't bad enough
that you brought that one"—he pointed to
Charley—"to the park?"

Thomas stood tall. "I did. I trust 'em, and you should,
too."

Deadnettle stared at him. Thomas stared right back
until the faery's shoulders drooped slightly. "All right.
This is in your hands—and on your head. What do we
do next?" He gestured to the hole in the wall. "There is
nowhere for us to go. He will find us wherever we are."

He asked the questions lightly, but Thomas could see it
wasn't so light as in his thoughts.

Deadnettle'd been luring him around, telling him what to do for days now, but he, Thomas, was the faery king. Wintercress's son, though he'd never known her. And Deadnettle had lured him out for a reason. Deadnettle's plans, his attempts, had failed. It was high time to do things a different way.

This whole time, Deadnettle had hastened to tell Thomas that the faeries were nothing like the stories told of them, that they were honest and gentle creatures. They didn't thieve babies from their cribs; they didn't thieve anything.

But stories, thought Thomas, couldn't get everything wrong, not always. And he had a hint, a flicker of memory . . .

"When you visited Silas and Lucy to give them the coins, did you leave anything else?" Thomas asked. "And why not simply put the coins in the grave with me?"

Deadnettle licked his lips. The split at the corner was still there, open and oozing. "I wanted to be sure they would take you in out of kindness alone, no matter what Wintercress's orders. In life, I had never defied her, but . . . But no, I left nothing else. We had nothing else to give you."

"Right. You lot stay here. We dug this now seeing as there might not be much time later. That spiritualist is prob'ly still sniffing around, and Mordecai might realize what's true, and there's that two-worlds business. If anything 'appens while we're gone, get out, go to the park, but we won't be long. Promise."

"Thomas, what are you planning?"

"I'll tell you if I'm right," said Thomas. "Seems to me . . . Seems to me you've been hoping about all the wrong things for too long. Just wait. I'm coming back," Thomas said to Silas. "Marigold, will you come too?"

"Of course."

It would be better to take Deadnettle, but Thomas could see himself the faery was still weakened from the iron chains, and Marigold was far more cheerful besides. Just in case Mordecai ventured down to the cellar again, unlikely as that seemed, the four of them made quick work of slotting the bricks back into place. They'd fall free at a push, but it was good enough to pass muster in the darkness. Thomas saved the split one for last, wedging each perfect half back into the gap with his fingertips. They crept up through the empty house, Marigold the most light-footed of all, her toes kicking up hardly any dust.

All the way to the river, Silas and Charley walked behind, carrying the shovels with their iron blades, but Marigold's pace slowed, and she tripped on the edges of the cobbles.

A *clank* rang over the water, the shovels banging together as Silas gave the two he carried to Charley and scooped Marigold up onto his back. Thomas stared.

"Don't gawp, lad. You'll catch flies."

Marigold giggled. "Thank you," she said, and Silas smiled gruffly.

"Never let it be said I wasn't a gentleman." He trotted ahead, making her laugh even harder, and Charley bumped his shoulder to Thomas's.

"'S not so bad, see?"

At the door of the house, Silas set Marigold gently to the ground again and gave her an odd, jerky little bow before opening the door.

"Oh!" said Lucy. Dark circles ringed her eyes. The clock tower at Westminster had struck three of the clock as they crossed the bridge. But that great bell was not a church bell, and Marigold had not stopped laughing at Silas. "And who might this be?"

"This is Marigold," Thomas said, but introductions were not the important thing now, manners or no. "You used to read to me at bedtime, 'fore I was old enough to take a shovel. You had a whole sheaf of faery stories."

Thomas had remembered this when *old ones, old ones, old ones* rang in his ears, back when he'd asked Charley what that meant. And Marigold, still a fledgling, looked as close to a normal girl as made a difference, but at a nod from Silas, Lucy's mouth opened. From a small shelf, torn cloth and cracked spines in a row, she took down a slim blue book.

"Where did you get it?"

Lucy set her hands to her hips and thought. "Now, you know, that's a strange tale in itself, if I's honest. We 'adn't found you yet, and I remember that, as it was so odd. I'd been out to market, you see, and stopped for a bit of a rest on my way back to cook Silas his supper. A woman came up, sat down next to me. Pretty, she was, with big eyes and long dark hair, as pretty as she was tall. I'd never seen a woman so tall as when she stood. And big with child, so's I was sure two would come out, like the Robertson girls, and told her so." Lucy's voice softened, remembering. "She asked me as I had any little ones, and I said no, but I hoped, perhaps . . . and she took that book from her sack and gave it right to me. Told me to read the stories to the son she was sure I'd have. And then, a month later . . . Oh, Thomas."

"Does that sound like her?" Thomas asked Marigold. "Like Wintercress?"

"As if it were Deadnettle speaking."

Thomas reached into his pocket. He couldn't recall when he'd stopped worrying they'd clink together, but two heavy silver faery coins sat in the bottom. He held one up to the firelight, the flames glinting off the face there. Lucy put her hand to her lips, nodded, turned away.

His finger already marked the tale he half remembered, but Thomas flipped the pages, thin as butterfly wings, to the front. He'd seen it, sometimes, in the other old books Lucy gathered for him to read and learn, bought for a ha'penny from a table at the market, messages from names he didn't recognize, belonging to folks he'd never meet.

The letters spiked across the page.

To the changeling, they said.

> Once upon a time, there was a human boy who lived between a great forest and a greater city. The city he could see growing even as he watched, taller and wider, as the forest shrank away, the trees cut down for firewood and timber. The last tree to be left standing was a strange one, indeed, and as the boy grew, he would sometimes go to sit in its shade on a hot day, leaning his back against the trunk.

> But, as I say, this was no ordinary tree. Sometimes two trees grow so close together that they join, and the only way it is possible to tell that it was once two trees and not one

is that there is a gap left at the bottom, and sometimes, this gap is large enough for a man to step through.

Without knowing why, one day, this was exactly what the boy did. He was nearly fully grown, nearly a man, and he had to push and squeeze his way through, the bark scraping at his skin and tearing his clothes. On the other side was not the field where the forest had once been, but a beautiful valley, with a beautiful river flowing at the bottom, and the most beautiful girl he had ever seen sitting on its bank. As he watched, the cuts on his arms healed, and he knew he was in a very magical place, indeed, and that the girl must be magic too, to live there.

He did not speak to her that day, or the next. He returned home, but every day he went back to visit, and soon the two spoke and fell in love. She wished him to stay in her land forever, where she was a princess, but he could not. There was work to be done, and so he took her back to his land instead.

They were happy for a time, though her skin was less pink, her eyes less bright than they had been when he had first seen her sitting by the water. She grew weary easily, poisoned by the iron all around, and when the church bells rang, they seemed to hurt her badly.

Because of this, the people called her a witch, or a demon, and claimed that she must have put a great magic on the boy to make him fall in love with her.

They had a child, and the people grew ever more worried that the child would grow to be like his mother. Desperate to prove that she was good, the girl had an iron ring forged and laid a spell upon it that would allow it to break any enchantment. She named it the Ring of Dispel, because such things need names, and called the people around to tell them of what she had done.

If he were truly in her power, the ring would set him free. She picked up the ring, but no sooner had she put it on his finger than the girl fell to the ground, never to rise again.

Thomas looked up from the page. Every one of the faeries was watching him. One or two wiped their eyes.

"I had heard the tale," said Deadnettle. "Her sister—Wintercress's mother—came through the gateway to learn what had become of her, and returned with the story. She used it as an excuse to seal the faery realm from humans, claimed no more would come and steal us away. Of course, that turned out not to be true. It was a very long time ago. Such things take on the stuff of legends, you know. It is far more likely that Hellebore simply touched iron for too long and died."

"Why wouldn't you believe her, if you can't tell lies?"

"Because she died soon after, and Wintercress became queen. I have heard it was assumed that the lie was what sickened her, too badly for even the faery realm to heal."

"So you don't think it's true?" Thomas asked. A rising hope ebbed away.

"I think it is . . . unlikely. And even if it were true, where would the ring be now? Long destroyed or lost. I have told you before: Do not believe the fables of us; they are never right."

"But this one might be," Thomas insisted. "If it wasn't, why did Wintercress leave me the book?"

The crack of Deadnettle's neck as he snapped his head to gaze at Thomas echoed around the cellar. "What did you say?"

"She left him the book, Deadnettle," said Marigold. "Gave it to Thomas's—to Lucy. Heard her myself. She described Wintercress, same as you always do. Or used to."

"When was this?" Deadnettle's eyes glowed in the gloom.

"A moon before you left Thomas on the grave."

A deathly hush fell over the room. Deadnettle paced back and forth, along the walls and across its width. Thomas couldn't figure what he was thinking, but he must've been thinking hard, to raise his hands to his head like that.

"Some of us did not survive the first year after the Summoning," Deadnettle whispered. "She told me she was dealing with our dead, as Mordecai permitted us to do. I tried to insist, but she said she was our queen and she had failed to protect us. That it was her task."

Thomas nodded. He understood that, right enough.

"And then she told me she was going to have a

hatchling, which takes a great deal of strength. Much more than for humans, so I understand. The process is much faster, and thus takes more energy, energy she did not have. I begged her to stay here and rest, but I could not watch her every moment. Mordecai made me take my hours in the cage."

"You didn't know what she was going to do with Thistle 'n me."

"No. And that spell took the very last of her strength, as I've said. But in the moments before she left us, when the one had become two, she made me promise to take you to Silas and Lucy. I was too distraught to ask her why. Why ensure you live at all—my apologies—or why they must be the ones to care for you. I simply did as she asked." Deadnettle strode the length of the cellar once more, and back again. "She must have had a purpose to it."

A quiet muttering rippled through the faeries, surprising Thomas enough that he looked away. He'd not heard them speak much. Other than when he'd first met them, they were always asleep, or near to it, or else just too hopeless to bother. Now they were agreeing that they'd always heard Wintercress to be wise and kind, never without reason.

It struck Thomas anew that not a one of them, save

Deadnettle, had known her. He could not ask them what she had been like. Same, he could not ask more than he had of the faery realm; Deadnettle had told him what he knew, but it was a whole land seen through only one pair of eyes.

"Deadnettle," said Marigold slowly. The book was folded open on her lap, and Thomas remembered that the first time he'd set eyes on her she'd had books then, too. She liked them. Her finger ran over the letters, reading the words easily as if they were written in the strange, spiky faery letters.

They were good with tongues, Deadnettle'd told him from the start. They had to be, for their mouths to form words in so many when the dead spoke through them.

Thomas shook himself and paid attention to Marigold. "Deadnettle, what would happen if a human tried to enter the faery realm? Now? Since it was sealed?"

"Why, they would die," said Deadnettle. It did not seem to bother him, the thought.

"And what if they didn't step through right away, but sort of . . . reached, to see what would happen? Especially if it were a man who had reason to think the realm might let him in."

"Why would they think that?" Deadnettle asked. And stopped. "They had a child. It likely had a child. On and on. By now there would be nearly no faery blood left in his veins, but he might think a drop was enough."

"I figure," said Thomas, casting his eyes between Deadnettle and Marigold and over the rest of the faeries, "I figure it'd turn his hand dead black, don't you?"

CHAPTER EIGHTEEN

Enemies Become Friends

D EADNETTLE CLIMBED THE STAIRS, THE poisonous iron nearing with every step. He could feel it, yes, on each window, each door. Mordecai had made quite certain. Even if the faeries had been willing to burn themselves to touch it, Mordecai would hear the screams long before they escaped.

No matter now. Lying made Deadnettle weak, but what he was sure was truth gave him strength. Up and up again to Mordecai's study.

He knocked. A crash came, a curse.

"Enter."

Ink spilled from the edge of Mordecai's desk, dripping livid blue to the rug. The fallen inkwell rocked back and forth over the wood, rhythmic, mesmerizing. Deadnettle looked away.

"Oh, it's you," said Mordecai, raising his blackened hand in a mockery of greeting. "I did not expect you. Are you not enjoying your rest? One would think you would be glad of it, though I must warn you, it will not last much longer. The plans I've made!"

"Indeed?" asked Deadnettle, clenching his pointed teeth to keep his face impassive.

"It will be miraculous." Mordecai stood, nearing Deadnettle but, as ever, not touching him. "The queen alone will keep me in riches beyond my wildest imaginings if we bring back the husband she so famously mourns. There won't be a soul in all of Britain who'll deny the power of our great Spiritualist works. Those who've lost loved ones will flock by the hundreds, the thousands, for my services. And the coins they bring shall be just as great in number."

"Miraculous," agreed Deadnettle mildly. "Tell me, Mordecai, how did you injure yourself?"

"An accident." Mordecai's words were clipped, chilled as the iron that barred the windows even here. "I do not see what that has to do with anything."

"Whereas I think it must be very important."

"Insolence!" The blackened hand rose and fell again

without striking. "Get back to your cellar, faery, and stay there."

"No. You see, I know your secret." Had not been the one to discover it, but knew it now, and that was enough. "Our land scorned you, didn't it, Mordecai? Humans are not permitted entrance, and that's what you are." Deadnettle spat, his spittle mixing with the ink on the floor. "Human."

Fury rose on Mordecai's face, a great, wild bird taking flight from a perch. "I am *not*. I am one of you! I deserved to return!"

"And yet . . ." Deadnettle pointed to Mordecai's hand.

It shook.

"Had you continued through, it would have killed you."

"It should have let me through," Mordecai hissed. "I am of faery blood just as you are. I did not know it—oh no, not at first, but I always knew I was special. Magical. I could feel it in my bones. And then, one day, I happened upon a story, a wonderful, fantastical story. I had traced my lineage, you see, and I know the names of my ancestors back through seven generations. And in this story, I found the name of a faery, a name one of my ancestors shared, and the name of the human she loved. And then, then, Deadnettle, I knew who I was, or could be." The sorcerer shut his mouth and looked around wildly, but it was too late. His anger and bitterness had poured out. He had said too much. Deadnettle smiled.

"But it did not work. You opened the gateway, but nothing more."

"It should have worked!" the sorcerer screamed. Deadnettle's head rang with the sound. Pictures in their frames rattled on the walls. "And when it didn't, I vowed revenge. And I got it, did I not? Oh, yes." The shouts transformed to laughter, wild laughter. "Far and wide I had to travel, but I learned what I needed to. The piles of ancient books I read, the number of wise magicians I sought . . ."

"To learn to summon us."

"There are spells. Enchantments. It was simpler than you might think."

"Tell me how."

All at once, Mordecai seemed to recover himself. He backed away from Deadnettle, shaking his head, a crazed smile stretching his lips. "I don't imagine I shall," he said. "Your mistake is believing that any of this changes the matter of your enslavement. You will still die here, Deadnettle, and the faery realm is home to no one. I will be glad to see you perish after I have gotten as much use from you as I can."

"Foul, evil—"

"That may be. Leave me now."

Deadnettle hurried out and down the stairs. Away from

the iron. Away so he could think. Had he told Mordecai that the faeries could not do that which Thomas had promised him they could, Deadnettle had no doubt the sorcerer would kill them where they stood.

But it would not be long before he discovered it. Thomas had gained them time and respite, but that would soon be over.

For the thousandth time—more, many more—he wished he could speak to Wintercress. Wintercress, who had kept secrets, even from him, to protect them.

How much had she known? Something, clearly, to have left the book for Thomas. How much had she simply guessed?

He was going out, he told the others. If Thomas and Marigold returned, they were to remain and wait for him. Deadnettle could get farther from the iron in the park now than he could at the Society. Only the odd lamppost to steer clear of, not bars and locks all around. They dutifully removed the bricks for him, and as he climbed the stairs of the elegant, ruined, empty house, he heard them scrape back into place.

The church bells struck as if physical blows upon his skin, through his long, dark cloak. Every scrap of iron he passed seemed to bend, to point directly at him, ready to skewer him through and through. Only when he reached the park did Deadnettle feel as if he could properly breathe again.

He looked up, concentrated. The leaves stayed still on their branches. Deadnettle tried to remember when he had last achieved a wisp of faery magic.

The note to Thomas. No, the breeze. And that had exhausted Deadnettle beyond reason.

"'Scuse me, sir?"

Deadnettle startled. A man stood on the path not far away. He was watching Deadnettle, but no fear or horror showed on his face. To be safe, Deadnettle drew the hood of his cloak tighter. "Yes?"

"D'you happen to know the time? Only I've lost my watch, you see, and my lady wife will not be best pleased if I'm late for supper."

"Oh." Deadnettle did not wear a watch, but pretended to look at one as he squinted into the distance, farther than a man could ever see. The great clock tower at Westminster stood tall over the river. "About five minutes before seven," he answered.

"Cheerio."

It did not occur to Deadnettle until the man was out of sight that a mere week before, he would simply have ignored him.

He'd meant to go to the hazel tree, to touch it if nothing else. The act gave him comfort, precious comfort. Instead,

Deadnettle walked slowly through the park, alive with the full flush of spring. Humans played and chattered and pushed their infants in those odd wheeled carts, smiling and laughing all the while.

They were not wholly foul, evil—

That part of the story was true. The part about the ring could well be, also, but Wintercress had left no clues as to how to find it. For that, Deadnettle had Mordecai to thank.

"A séance, Deadnettle? Truly?"

He nodded to Marigold. "How many times have you or I been summoned to the cage so that someone may learn where their dead relative hid the gold brooch or priceless hair ornament or, yes, a ring? Mordecai has made his fortune off such pettiness. These are our gifts, Marigold; I see no reason we should not use them. But we shall need a human."

"Why?"

"Because according to the tale, a human was the last to have it. Thus, our best chance at knowing where it lies now."

Thomas opened his mouth and closed it again. A rare smile reopened the wound on Deadnettle's lip that stubbornly refused to heal; he felt the dark blood drip down. How easily the boy forgot.

"Lucy or Silas'd do it," said Thomas. "Charley, too. Wait. No. I know who's we should ask."

"Oh?" Deadnettle waited, but Thomas simply grinned, innocent and mischievous. He was yet so young. "Back in a tick."

It was longer than that, but when Thomas returned, the smile remained fixed firmly on the face so like Thistle's. It seemed to Deadnettle, however, that in the short time since he had set eyes on Thomas, his features had changed. Older, now, with a shrewdness and cunning Thistle had never possessed.

"Let's go," Thomas said.

Marigold skipped after him, full of energy since the weight of her secret had been lifted. Deadnettle followed them both, wondering how Thomas could be both the faery king and such a foolish child in the same moment. He was enjoying his little mystery, smiling as he took Marigold by the hand and whirled her around a corner.

When they had been walking a full half hour, Deadnettle stopped to rest against a wall, the red brick digging into his back. He wished he could suggest that they hail a hansom, but they were bound about with iron and pulled by horses who did their best to bolt whenever they sensed one of Deadnettle's kind.

"Are you all right?" Marigold asked.

"Yes." The answer was painful, but there was nothing anymore that was not. Hope itself was painful now, the feeling renewed, strong, acute. It nearly balanced the iron sting, the blows of the bells. Nearly. Tangled with the large hope that Thomas was sure of what he was doing was the smaller one that they would not have to walk much farther to achieve it.

In fact, it was a whole half hour again, Deadnettle lagging behind Thomas and Marigold as they chattered. She was telling him more about the faery realm she'd never seen, everything she had ever heard. How easily they had become friends, but that was not such a surprise, perhaps. To her, he was a copy of Thistle, and to him, well, it didn't sound as if the boy had grown up with many his own age. There was Charley, who had helped dig the hole in the wall, but Deadnettle knew of no others.

The faeries had always had that, at least. Too much closeness, arguably, but they had always been together. Among their own. Thomas, neither one thing nor another, had nobody in any world about whom he could say the same.

Why did you make me do it, Wintercress? We could have dealt with the changeling another way. What did you know?

His question rose and swooped silently with the birds overhead, iridescent black, but no answer came. It never did.

Thomas turned yet another corner, into a short,

shadowed lane. He stopped at a doorway and stood beside a small sign. Marigold clapped. Deadnettle read it. *Oh, you clever boy,* he thought for the second time in as many days. A risk, yes, but one that now felt worth taking. The cut on his lip split again, and vengeance dripped from his long, pointed teeth.

Mordecai had no maids, no servants of any kind, nor any wife to help him. Often, Deadnettle had heard his visitors express surprise when Mordecai hung up their coats and hats himself, his good hand reaching for the hooks on the walls. A gray-haired woman, thin as a rail, showed them in and led them up creaking, rickety stairs, her worn shoes rubbing threadbare carpet. She seated them in the cramped space at the top on mismatched chairs, her eyes passing over Deadnettle's cloaked figure as if he were not the strangest thing she'd seen even this very day.

"He will be with you shortly," she said, and disappeared down a corridor.

Deadnettle felt as if he had walked longer than an hour, so far was this place from the splendor of the Society. Voices came from the other side of the thin wall behind his head; with some effort, he chose not to listen. It did not matter whether the man was not a fraud, which of course he was. Deadnettle, Marigold, and Thomas could take care of that.

A short while later, a weeping lady fled through the room and down the stairs, her eyes so blurred with tears that she didn't see the shrouded man and two children she passed. Water poured from a jug and was gulped from a glass. The door handle turned once more.

"A good afternoon to you. Please enter." A young man, no more than five-and-twenty, stood over them. "Do I know you, young man? You look familiar."

That voice. Yes, it was the right man. Thomas stood, tugging Marigold with him. Deadnettle felt the man's eyes rove over his cloak and heard the faint tremor in the next words. "How can I be of service? Do you wish to contact a dear, departed one?"

"We need to find something," said Thomas. "And in payment, we will give you something you want, and more silver coins than you can count, besides."

"Oh?" Curiosity radiated. "I hardly know what to ask first: What it is you seek, or what it is you think I desire."

From the shadow of his hood, Deadnettle gazed about the room. Thick curtains covered the one window. Small lamps burned on tables. Some sort of device that could be operated by a foot pedal was half-hidden beneath a table. A crystal ball glowed like a faery eye on a tarnished stand. Rooms such as this littered London; none were like Mordecai's. Here there was no cage. There were secrets, yes, and lies, too, but not one as dreadful, as cruel as the sorcerer's.

"We wish to find a ring."

"Aha," said the man to Thomas. "A common request. I am pleased to tell you I have assisted in many such matters." There was no hint of pain at the lie. How easily humans did it. "Sir, do you not wish to remove your cloak? You must be very warm."

Deadnettle ignored him. So did Thomas. "You wish to discover Mordecai's secret," Thomas continued. The man's eyes widened. He looked from Thomas to Marigold and peered at Deadnettle as if hoping he would suddenly be able to see through the thick cloth.

"Help us, Jensen," Deadnettle said, speaking for the first time. A twitch of the arm, and his cloak dropped away.

CHAPTER NINETEEN

The Path of Faery Letters

J ENSEN WENT WHITE WITH SHOCK, pale as a faery. Thomas near laughed at Deadnettle. That'd been a decent bit of theater, better than the tumblers and ventriloquists in the music hall.

"What *are* you?"

"We are called by many names," Deadnettle said, and Thomas heard the chant in his mind. *Old ones, old ones, old ones.*

"What do you know of a ring called the Ring of Dispel?" Thomas asked, paying no mind to Jensen's question.

"I . . . Ah. That is, yes, anyone interested in the Mysteries knows of it. An old tale. Very old. There are many versions, but the thread of the story remains the same. Given to a human by the queen of the fae—" His face went, if anything, even more bloodless. "It cannot be."

"It is," said Thomas. "He's been keeping 'em locked up, prisoners! Making 'em weak and sick and dying!"

"You shall have to tell me everything," said Jensen, pointing to the chairs around the table with a trembling hand.

They did. Thomas filled in what bits he could, but mostly it was Deadnettle and Marigold. All about being dragged through the gateways and locked in cages when they weren't in the horrid cellar, and the iron and the bells. Jensen rose when Deadnettle reached that part, and moved every bit of the metal from the room.

"Tell me about the other one," said Jensen when he returned, looking at Deadnettle but pointing at Thomas. "How is it possible?"

Deadnettle opened his mouth, as did Marigold, but it was Thomas who spoke first. "Magic created us," he said, "and I never got to meet 'im, but I think he was just a boy, like me. He was just trying to do what his elders bade him, and what was best for his family. He was wrong, and all right, maybe it didn't work such treat, but I dunno if being wrong was his fault. Not when the whole thing was never his idea in the first place. Where I'm from, folks try to scrape by every day, and do the best they can. It's what Lucy 'n Silas do, and it's what I did until I met this lot. Still am, p'raps. So I reckon, I reckon Thistle was mostly like me. He could do a few things I can't, but I can do a few things *he* couldn't, so there. Maybe if we'd ever been in the same place at once, we'd've been like a whole person. Like them twins who finish each other's words an' that."

"You forgot clever," Deadnettle added mildly. "Both of you."

"And very brave," said Marigold.

Thomas felt his cheeks heat.

"Well," said Jensen. "I never imagined. I knew Mordecai had some secret, some knowledge he would not impart to the rest of us, but this is cruelty beyond what I would have thought even him capable of. I apologize, on behalf of us humans, for what you have been forced to endure. You may think me a charlatan, an impostor"—his foot hit the pedal of an odd device beneath the table, and a series of muffled raps sounded—"and you would be correct. But my interest in what is beyond our limited vision has always been real. You must explain one more thing, however."

Thomas waited. Deadnettle sat with his hands folded upon the tablecloth, and Marigold leaned forward. "If we were to locate the ring, and how I would like to, not only for Mordecai's defeat but to right such grievous wrongs done to your kind, how will you use it? I saw with my own eyes your relief when I removed the iron."

It seemed weeks, months, years ago that Thomas had been frustrated by not being able to ruffle the leaves on the trees. He straightened his shoulders. "Thomas is a very special kind of faery," said Marigold. "He will save us."

The room was cleared of near everything save the table and chairs and one of the lamps. Jensen's tools and tricks to fool the humans who came to call upon him weren't needed here, and Deadnettle said it helped to be free of any distraction. Jensen wasn't half-thirsty, stopping to drink two glasses of water from the jug and calling to the gray-haired woman for more. Thomas's stomach shook with a whole storm of butterflies. It was all very well for Marigold to say he'd save 'em, and he would, too, but he'd not done this bit before. Marigold telling him all about what it was like didn't feel the same, in the face of it.

Furious whispers came from the corner. Thomas left Jensen rolling up his sleeves and neared, listening to the argument.

"I am more experienced."

"And I am stronger."

"All the more reason. You know the difficulties of this, Marigold. I would be less of a loss."

"Nothing will happen, Deadnettle. Let Thomas choose."

"He cannot possibly know—"

"Let me choose what?"

The faeries faced him, young and old. "The longer a person has been gone, the more difficult it is to reach them," said Deadnettle. "The more dangerous for us. Marigold and I were *discussing* which of us should allow him passage into this world so that he might answer our question."

Oh.

Thomas didn't want to choose; Deadnettle was right. How was he supposed to know which of 'em would be better at it? But he, Thomas, had promised to save them. He was their faery king, though he could do none of the things they could do. He could do things they could not, and that made him, as Marigold said, a very special kind of faery. True, Deadnettle might've thought at first that he could just boss Thomas about, tell him what to do and he'd do it, and maybe Thomas'd done it at first too.

But not now.

"You can do it?" he asked Marigold.

"Of course."

Jensen cleared his throat. The three of them turned to him.

"I am afraid I do not know what to do next. My previous customers have been content—or perhaps not—with whatever show I put on for them, but I suspect it is you who will be putting one on for me this time."

The butterflies in Thomas's stomach urgently flapped their wings. Deadnettle set a chair a little ways from the table, muttering that it was far preferable to a cage and, clearly bested, gestured Marigold to it.

"You will have to ask her to bring you the keeper of the iron ring. Ask for the ring by name, as we do not know for certain the name of the one who held it last. It may take some time for the spirit to appear; she will have to search far back across the ages."

Thomas, Deadnettle, and Jensen took their seats at the table, their faces turned to Marigold. Jensen patted his forehead with a handkerchief far finer than his suit.

"Ready," said Marigold, and closed her eyes. Another gulp of water, and Jensen spoke.

Nothing happened, bar a hush falling over the room. And then, then it swirled and thickened until Thomas tasted fog on his tongue. Marigold's large eyes flickered under their lids. The lamp flame dipped and stretched, casting shadows across the room. Thomas thought for a moment that Jensen had put his foot on the pedal of his device, but it was the shutters tapping outside the window. *Tap, tap, tap, SLAM.*

When they had walked here, there had been no wind. It howled now, screaming down the lane outside as if trying to get away as fast as it could. More screams came, human ones, paired with footsteps running down the stairs and a door slamming below.

Blood ran cold in Thomas's veins. His teeth chattered. Deadnettle's knuckles clenched the arms of his chair. The thick dark hairs on Jensen's head stood straight on end.

In her chair, Marigold shook and shook, her teeth bared. Pain twisted across her face, and Thomas felt Deadnettle's hand clamp down on his shoulder, pushing him back to his seat. Marigold's eyes snapped open.

"We seek the ring known as the Ring of Dispel!" Jensen shouted. "Tell us where to search!"

Marigold spoke with a voice that was not her voice, and tumbled sideways to the floor.

Silence. But it did not feel like silence, with the crash of Marigold's body still echoing through Thomas's head. He reached her an instant before Deadnettle, two before Jensen.

Thomas had seen far more death than most. She lived, but it was a close thing.

"Wake up!" he shouted, slapping her face.

But she did not.

"Is this usual?" Jensen demanded, but he could see Deadnettle's fear plain as Thomas could. "Oh dear. But we . . . we . . ."

"Do shut up!" said Deadnettle. "Marigold. Oh,

Marigold." The old faery whirled around, and Thomas'd never seen such a wild stare. "We must get her home. Do you understand? Not to the Society. *Home*."

Home. The faery realm. A place of great healing, Deadnettle had told him. And at the time, he had spoken of it with longing clearly for himself.

"It is the only thing that might save her now. We have no time, Thomas. Do whatever you must. You heard what was said, yes? Go! Now! You"—he pointed at Jensen—"will you assist me?"

Thomas ran. Down the stairs and down the lane and into a hansom before the cabbie could get so much as an eyeful of him. The horse reared and kicked and neighed, rocking the carriage so hard that Thomas was thrown from one side to the other. He yelled to the driver and heard the crack of the whip as frantic hooves took off down the busy street.

Marigold. She had been so kind to him. Sure, part of it was him being the spitting image of Thistle, but she'd liked him for himself, too, and helped him where she could.

The carriage teetered on two wheels around a corner, and another. Soon—not soon enough!—it clattered over a bridge. "I wants paying, scamp," shouted the driver, panting as he fought the nag to a standstill. The cracked cobbles wobbled underfoot when Thomas jumped down.

He tossed a whole silver faery coin up, watching it flip over and over through the air into the outstretched hand.

"Cor! Wot's this, then?"

Thomas ran inside. A clang echoed, the pot Lucy had been scrubbing tossed aside.

He let her embrace him, but there was no time, no time for this. "Where's Silas?"

"Why, Silas's out, poppet. Didn't say where. You know 'im. I'd imagine Charley is off sailing those wee boats of his, if 'e'd be a help?"

Thomas took a breath for what felt the first time since Marigold'd fallen. Warm, comforting scents gathered around him. "The faery girl I brought here is proper ill," he said. "I need to save her. I need to save them all."

Lucy reached out to cup his cheek with a rough, reddened hand. "They's asked a lot of you, ain't they?"

Yes. But then again, no. Thomas didn't like to think of what he'd try to escape a rake like Mordecai. And in turn, they had shown him who he was. What he was.

"Please," he said, "please go find Charley. Silas . . . It's fine. Leave him. But find Charley. Tell him he's to go to where we went before and get them out. There's a hazel tree in the very middle of the big park at Westminster. He knows where it is." He felt behind the door, fingers closing around the familiar handle.

Wintercress had told Deadnettle precisely where to leave Thomas. She'd left him a book, though he'd never known it. Thomas walked south, leaving the rushing of the river far behind, eyes darting back and forth. South, then west, toes pointing to where, long ago, the faery realm had lain over this one. It was miles away, 'course, hundreds of miles, but Thomas knew this was right. Not even faery vision would be looking hard as he was, in case she'd left him anything else.

There. Etched into a low wall, gray and crumbling, the spikes and whorls near faded to nothing.

They said, *This way.*

Thomas kept on, past the houses and shops and filthy slums.

Keep going.

He had to search and search for the next, pushing aside overgrown brambles that scratched his hands to blood. The letters were more jagged, sloppier, as if she had been overtired when she'd carved them.

This is as much as I know.

He cocked his head to the side, puzzled and puzzling. What'd she mean, this was as much as she knew? Thomas wanted to sit, to think, but Marigold . . .

His steps quickened instead, to the next road, dodging the carts and barrows to the other side. Foot raised to step to the curb, Thomas felt something wash over him. It wasn't pain, not so's he'd call it, but . . . odd. Like a thousand little spider legs scrabbling over his skin. He moved back and forth. The spiders fled and returned and fled again as Thomas moved. Puzzled, he stepped away and held out an arm, feeling the tingle crawl up to the elbow.

The barrier, the one that kept the faeries trapped. He could feel it, yes, but he could also step through it.

Curious. Deadnettle might like to know, though Thomas hoped it soon wouldn't matter, and neither Deadnettle nor any of the other faeries would need to concern themselves with anything whatsoever in the human realm once they were back in their own.

"Oi! You! What you doing in the street, boy?"

He was less worried by such voices than he'd once been. "None of your business, so mind it!" he shouted back.

"Why, you—"

Thomas began to run. He knew the graveyard ahead, beyond the magical barrier with which Mordecai trapped the faeries in London. He'd been there with Silas many a night, shovel over his shoulder just as it was now. Night was falling, but slowly, the sun reluctant to give way to the sliver of moon.

But light enough to read the stones by, as he'd always done, marking their names. Thomas grasped the iron gates and pushed.

CHAPTER TWENTY

Find Your Bones

I T WAS TIME TO FIND his bones.

And once again, they were truly his—bone and blood and family. Here, in this place, where the human man had buried the faery woman he loved so that he might remain close to her. Over the grass and along the paths, he moved through the graves, quickly enough for Marigold, slowly enough to read the names.

He'd always been comfortable in graveyards.

"Where are you?" he whispered.

Here, answered a voice in his head. *Come and find me. Come and speak to me.*

Thomas spun, twisting an ankle, and saw. Burning pain shot up his leg, but he ran regardless, down toward the very edge and the hazel tree that grew all funny, two trees really, joined together with a space between. A single grave rested beneath, its stone so worn he could scarce make out anything in the dusk. Wouldn't have been able to if he hadn't known exactly what he was looking for.

"Hellebore," he read from the whorled, spiked letters.

Greetings.

"Hold up." The shovel's blade hovered an inch above the overgrown mass of weeds that tangled across the plot. "You can hear me."

Yes.

"But—"

But the moon was rising in the sky, pulling the faery realm farther away. He would ask Deadnettle about this later, if he got a second's chance. He had to hurry!

"Will this hurt you?" The iron glinted dully.

Not any longer.

He began to dig.

And dig.

And dig.

Whoever'd buried her hadn't wanted to make it easy. Six feet he dug, then eight. Muscles ached and calluses burned. At the ninth, blade struck bone, her shroud long since rotted away. Thomas put the shovel far away against a tree and climbed down, scrabbling at the wall of the hole, tearing fingernails on rocks and twigs caught in the earth.

He had to be so careful now.

It was in my hand.

Inch by inch, Thomas found his bones, loose and tumbling through his fingers. He sifted through the soil, feeling, gripping every likely thing between thumb and forefinger before dropping it and moving on to the next.

This? No. Not that or that, either. He didn't look at what he was touching, just moved from bone to bone.

It had fallen from her hand, no great surprise. Under a last surviving scrap of rotten cloth, Thomas's fist closed around the iron ring.

"Thank you," Thomas said, holding it up to the moonlight. "Thank you."

Be careful, said Hellebore. *Touching it brought me to my death, but you have not joined me yet. I wish you luck.*

It tingled as Thomas slipped it over his finger, tingled as the barrier had done, not with pain, but with magic. Faery magic. Hand over fist, he clawed himself from the grave and looked down into it. He would return to cover her. She would understand that now there was no time. He must get back to Marigold and the others.

As was the way of such things, it felt as if returning took less time than the finding, and he was lighter now. He'd left the shovel, but the iron ring weighed heavy on his finger.

He was gasping when he reached the gates to the park. Blood dripped from his hands, unnoticed before now, the cuts he had made in the last attempt reopened and weeping. Dizzied, he could not remember when he had last had a wink of sleep, and he was tired. So tired he felt as if he should like to sleep forever.

Soon enough. Not much farther now.

Deep in the park, the hazel tree stood tall. Through the gap, a distant lamp winked. The faeries were gathered, shielded in their cloaks with Charley and Jensen before them, and one on the ground, motionless as death.

"Stay back!" Thomas ordered, holding up his hand, the ring a black line darker than the night. "Is she alive?"

"Barely," answered Deadnettle, but his shoulders slumped in relief. "You have it. We are going home." His head tilted to look at the moon, pointed teeth bared in a smile.

"If it works."

"Do you know what to do?"

Thomas didn't, but he knew who would. She had been trying to help him all along, speaking in his sleep, dreams he scarcely remembered when he awoke. But he was awake now, and he knew he could do another thing the other faeries could not.

"Wintercress," he said, concentrating. "Help me."

He waited for her voice. Waited and waited. And when one came, it was not hers. One of the faeries stepped forward and drew back the hood of its cloak with a dead, charred hand.

"So close and yet so far," Mordecai said with a wicked grin. "Did you think I would let you leave?"

Charley stumbled as Mordecai pushed him out of the way. Deadnettle caught him by the arm.

"It doesn't hurt me any more than it hurts you." Mordecai came closer, closer to the iron ring around Thomas's finger. It felt cold and dull and heavy. "We are much the same, young changeling. I did not realize what you were, at first. I believed until recently your fanciful story that you had been brought back from the dead. But then I remembered a tale, an old tale, handed down as my own was, of one such as you, made before the two worlds were forced apart. I am amazed Wintercress achieved it; I thought I had weakened her enough."

"You hadn't," said Thomas coldly. "Here I am."

"And here you'll stay. You, none of you, will see your rightful home again." Mordecai raised his arms.

Fear struck through Thomas like lightning, like bells. "Help me," he whispered again.

The word came to him in his head. Jackrabbit quick, far faster than the sorcerer expected, Thomas pushed him aside and ran through the cluster of faeries, cut hands slamming to the bark of the tree, blood and iron meeting the wood as he screamed the spell in the ancient faery tongue.

The moon flickered. The world shook.

And the gateway opened.

"No!" Mordecai roared. Fingers closed around Thomas's throat, squeezing, squeezing. He felt the faeries try to pull him free, but Mordecai's grip was too tight, and they were too weak. Spots danced before Thomas's eyes.

He had no clue what'd happen, but there was nothing else for it.

Thomas stepped through the gap.

CHAPTER TWENTY-ONE

Homes

THOMAS MARSDEN WAS TWELVE YEARS old when he succeeded in opening the gateway to the faery realm.

The grip on his throat loosened straightaway. He heard Mordecai fall with a thud behind him. Heard, but not saw. A gray mist surrounded him, a fog like soup, too thick to squint through.

Other sounds came. Voices. "Thomas," said Deadnettle, and Thomas felt the weight of a hand on his shoulder. "You did it."

"Doesn't look like much to me. This fog'd put London to shame." Relief bubbled through him as laughter. "This is your wonderful faery realm?"

"It is yours, too. Perhaps more yours than anyone's."

"But I'm not a faery, not truly. Not like one of you. I can't see a blind thing in here, and I'll reckon you can see for miles."

"That isn't what I meant, which I suspect you knew." A hint of a smile graced Deadnettle's voice, and warmth flushed through Thomas. "You have a particular kind of human mind. Cunning and guile most of us do not possess, although I think too much time reading books has made Marigold cleverer than she perhaps needs to be."

Thomas laughed. Elsewhere, the faeries were laughing too, joyful and bubbling.

"You think of things as a human does, Thomas," Deadnettle continued. "Faced with the problem of the gateway, Wintercress sought a solution of magic, of blood. Faced with the problem of a locked door, you sought an iron tool with which to smash it down. You are very human, but you are very much a faery, too. And you are our faery king."

Thomas stared down at shoes he couldn't see. "Dunno about all that," he mumbled. "Well, p'raps the king part. That has a certain something."

It was Deadnettle's turn to laugh. A strong, healthy laugh.

"Please do something for me. Sit, just here. Sit and wait."

Deadnettle helped him to the soft grass.

"What's s'posed to happen?"

"I am not certain. It's been so long, and never like this..."

Thomas curled his hands, gasped. "I'm still wearing the ring. Here! Move back!"

"It's all right. Wait."

Too weary to argue, Thomas waited. One by one, or so he assumed, the faeries came and touched the top of his head, big hands and small ones. His eyes closed of their own accord, as if the iron was sapping his strength to keep them open, like the faeries in the cellar for so long. His head felt full up, of the past few days and everything that had happened, and a hundred thousand memories...

Memories that were not his. Cellars and cages and a night when everything went dark.

He opened his eyes.

It was as beautiful as Deadnettle had always told him, fields and valleys and a wide blue river.

"A place of great healing," said Deadnettle calmly, and Thomas remembered the fortune-teller. *Broken.*

"I am... both halves again? Fixed?"

"Very nearly stitched back together. I could not be sure, but I hoped. And I believe Wintercress knew. I believe she knew everything, and kept it from me to keep us safe. If Mordecai had asked the wrong questions, which is to say, the right questions, we would have been in such danger. More than we were."

"Did you know?" Thomas asked. He did not say it to Deadnettle.

You have realized what else you can do that the others cannot, said Wintercress. The words swept through his head like a voice in a dream.

"I can speak to you," he said.

You can. A gift given only to rare, precious changelings. And yes, Thomas, I knew. I knew you would save us, and you now have some of the magic of our kind and some that is entirely your own.

"Wintercress," whispered Deadnettle, and Thomas wished, for an instant, that he could pull the voice from his head and put it inside the old faery's. But only for an instant. She was his, and he had a great deal to ask her. The idea of speaking to the dead, or rather, letting them answer, no longer seemed as repulsive as it once had.

Tell him I am happy.

Thomas did. The last of the shadows of worry and pain faded from Deadnettle's face as Thomas watched.

"I could stay here."

"Indeed, you could."

A movement caught the corner of his eye. Marigold skipped over, smiling. "You should! We'd have such fun." She paused. "Thistle?" she asked quietly.

"Yes?" It was Thomas who spoke.

She gazed at him for a long, long time. Thomas saw tears welling at the corners of her eyes, yet she still smiled, as she almost always had, every time he'd seen her.

"I miss you," she said. "But I like Thomas better."

Too right, thought Thomas. He would miss her, too, a great deal, but he could not stay here. On the other side of the doorway was Charley, his friend for near as long as he—or part of him, leastways—had known Marigold. There was work to be done, not least covering Hellebore in her grave again. And despite Deadnettle's assurances, he wanted to take the iron away. Pushing himself to his feet, he walked to the hazel tree. "I'll come back to visit," he promised, and stepped through.

The world seemed exactly as he'd left it. Jensen and Charley waited.

"And here, too?"

Anywhere you like.

Some of the magic of the faeries and some of his own. He turned the iron ring on his finger. It was a funny old world, wasn't it, and there was more than one of 'em. He'd seen no end of strangeness in his life, that being a hazard of grave digging, but nothing would ever be so odd as these past days. His accidental afterlife was over and ahead lay his future one, ready to be filled to the brim like a glass of the freshest, cleanest water. Well, he had a proposal for Jensen, one that would make them both richer than Mordecai. He'd be able to buy Lucy all the onions she needed, and Silas'd never have to lift a shovel again.

Nor would Thomas. For he had found his bones.